MY CUPCAKE "A DAILY TASTY TRE

"Open your mouth and taste, open your eyes and see – how good God is. Blessed are you who run to him!"
Psalm 34:8(MSG)

My Cupcake – "A DAILY TASTY TREAT" Devotional

By Denise Rochelle Wright

DeniseRochelle

2021

Copyright © 2021 by Denise Rochelle Wright

All rights reserved. Except as permitted under the U.S. Copyright Act of 1976, no part of this publication may be reproduced, distributed, or transmitted in any form or by any means, or stored in a database or retrieval system, without the prior written permission of the publisher.

Scriptures quotations noted AMP are from The Amplified Bible. Copyright 1954, 1958, 1962, 1964, 1965, 1987, by the Lockman Foundation. All rights reserved. Used by permission. (www.Lockman.org)

Scriptures quotations noted NKJV are taken from the New King James Version, Copyright 1979, 1980, 1982 by Thomas Nelson, Inc., Publishers.

Scriptures quotations noted The Message are taken from The Message. Copyright 1993, 1994, 1995, 1996, 2000, 2001, 2002. Used by permission of NavPress Publishing Group

http://biblia.com/bible/ncv

http://biblia.com/bible/message

http://biblia.com/bible/nkjv

2015 Daily Devotional

First Printing: 2021

ISBN 978-1-099-82073-1

The Voice of Encouragement

Dedication

To my beautiful grandmother Mrs. Annie Louise Ford Herring who raised me from six weeks old. At an early age, my grandmother taught me about God, how to pray, love and the meaning of family. She was never just 'my grandmother', but my guardian, my friend, and my inspiration. The love of a grandma is extraordinary. God must have given grandmothers to us to liven up our lives, to make our lives more complete, make us well rounded, and better human beings. Thank you, grandma, for your sacrifices, care, concern, love, and everything that you did for me. I am forever grateful and thankful that you were my grandmother. Your spirit lives on in me and in all those you touched by your love, strength, wisdom, and beauty. You truly were a special, special woman! Miss you so much and Love you forever grandma.

Introduction

In the Bible, you will find a solution for just about every problem you face in life. How often have you gone for help to a pastor, counselor, or friend only to have them direct you back to the scriptures? When you get sick enough, you will not argue with the doctor, you will just take the medicine! Paul writes, "When you received His message from us, you didn't think of our words as mere human ideas. You accepted what we said as the very word of God which of course, it is. And this word continues to work in you who believe." God's Word works when you work it! But it only "continues to work in you who believe." So, do not read it and then go out and say something different; get into agreement with God. Let His word on the issue be your word on it too! The Amplified Bible says, "The Word of God, which is effectually at work in you who believe [exercising its superhuman power in those who adhere to and trust in and rely on it]" (1 Thessalonians 2:13 AMP). One day an unbeliever said to a believer that it was quite impossible to believe in any book whose author was unknown. The believer asked him if the compiler of the multiplication table was known. "No," he answered. "Then of course, you don't accept it?" the believer asked. The skeptic replied, "Oh yes, I believe in it because it works well." The believer replied, "So does the Bible." The greatest investment you can make in yourself is reading and studying your Bible. An unknown poet wrote: "Though the cover is worn, and the pages are torn, and though places bear traces of tears. Yet more precious than gold is this book worn and old, that can shatter and scatter my fears. When I prayerfully look in this precious old book, as my eyes scan the pages I see; Many tokens of love from the Father above, who is nearest and dearest to me. This old book is my guide, 'tis a friend by my side, it will lighten and brighten my way. And each promise I find soothes and gladdens my mind, as I read it and heed it today." Whatever you must sacrifice, whatever priorities you must rearrange, read your Bible daily.

It is one thing to hear how God works based on someone else experience, it is another to see it first-hand in your own life. I have learned through personal experiences; it is in the fire that I discover new aspects of God's care and character. I also learned what turns worthless carbon into diamonds is heat and pressure! The most important thing, while in the fire I discovered, when everyone abandoned me God remained faithful and is still faithful. Jesus is a friend and will never ever leave you; trust me I know this personally.

I have written this devotional book of encouragement so you can be encouraged daily! My prayer is that you will take just a moment each day to bless your future with one of these inspirational and positive encouragements. I believe you will put yourself in a position for God to move mighty. What God is about to do in your life will shock some people, amaze others, and upset many! The words you speak determine the way you live. Speaking God's promises can bring about His amazing blessing. There is incredible power in words.

My Cupcake "A Daily Tasty Treat" Devotional

Day 1 – Exodus 33:11-17 (MSG)

In God's Presence

11 And GOD spoke with Moses face-to-face, as neighbors speak to one another. When he would return to the camp, his attendant, the young man Joshua, stayed—he did not leave the Tent. 12-13 Moses said to GOD, "Look, you tell me, 'Lead this people,' but you don't let me know whom you're going to send with me. You tell me, 'I know you well and you are special to me.' If I am so special to you, let me in on your plans. That way, I will continue being special to you. Don't forget, this is your people, your responsibility." 14 GOD said, "My presence will go with you. I'll see the journey to the end." 15-16 Moses said, "If your presence doesn't take the lead here, call this trip off right now. How else will it be known that you're with me in this, with me and your people? Are you traveling with us or not? How else will we know that we're special, I and your people, among all other people on this planet Earth?" 17 GOD said to Moses: "All right. Just as you say, this also I will do, for I know you well and you are special to me. I know you by name."

Just an Observation

"My Presence will go with you, and I will give you rest" Exodus 33:14 NIV. Unless you spend time in God's presence you will always have an underlying sense of insecurity. There are certain people we draw security from just by being around them; their presence and approach to life make us feel better. Likewise, when you need to be lifted and strengthened you must spend time with God. In my opinion, being in His presence is like being in a room filled with perfume; you take the fragrance of it with you when you leave. Moses spent a great deal of time with God. He knew that without God's presence he was not worth two cents. Can you imagine being responsible for the daily care of two million people and getting them out of one country into another on foot? It is mind-boggling. And as if that weren't bad enough, the Israelites spent much of their time complaining and finding fault with Moses. When things went wrong, he was their favorite target. It was an ideal situation for losing your mind. But God told Moses, "My Presence will go with you, and I will give you rest." God can give you rest during trouble and peace, in the midst of conflict. God's presence can help you to show love in the face of mistreatment, and patience in times of stress. It can help you to bring positive change without a lot of words and end up feeling good about the way you handled things. So, spend time in God's presence today, its life changing.

Day 2 – Isaiah 42:16 (NIV)

Embracing CHANGE

I will lead the blind by ways they have not known, along unfamiliar paths I will guide them; I will turn the darkness into light before them and make the rough places smooth. These are the things I will do; I will not forsake them.

Just an Observation

 "Along unfamiliar paths I will guide them" Isaiah 42:16 NIV. Change forces us out of the comfort of the familiar and into the discomfort of the unfamiliar. While it can turn our world upside down, it makes us face our greatest fears and deal with the things that steal our joy, peace, and confidence. Change can be your friend or foe, depending on how you use it. Running away turns it into an enemy; embracing and learning from it makes it one of your greatest allies. Author C. Neil Strait said: "Change is always hardest for the man who's in a rut for he has scaled down his living to that which he can handle comfortably and welcomes no change or challenge that would lift him up." When you are facing the unknown, instead of automatically going into resistance mode, "Fix your eyes on what lies before you…stay on the safe path" (Proverbs 4:25-26 NLT). Ask yourself: What is God trying to teach me? How can I become stronger and wiser? What opportunities does it hold? Author John Mason stated, "Correction and change always result in fruit…One change makes way for the next, giving you the opportunity to grow. Every time you think you're ready to graduate from the school of experience, someone thinks up a new course…If you can figure out when to stand firm and when to bend, you've got it made." We do not have to fear what lies ahead. "Along unfamiliar paths I will guide them; I will turn the darkness into light before them and make the rough places smooth…I will not forsake them" (Isaiah 42:16). God never closes a door without opening another one—but you must be willing to walk through it.

My Cupcake "A Daily Tasty Treat" Devotional

Day 3 – Deuteronomy 20:1-4 (MSG)

Trust

1-4 When you go to war against your enemy and see horses and chariots and soldiers far outnumbering you, do not recoil in fear of them; GOD, your God, who brought you up out of Egypt is with you. When the battle is about to begin, let the priest come forward and speak to the troops. He'll say, "Attention, Israel. In a few minutes you're going to do battle with your enemies. Don't waver in resolve. Don't fear. Don't hesitate. Don't panic. GOD, your God, is right there with you, fighting with you against your enemies, fighting to win."

Just an Observation

Christians face battles every day, struggling with health, relationships, and finances. Some accept defeat before the battle is won. How does one keep focus when facing the enemy? Trust in the Lord, for He fights alongside believers to ensure their victory. The Lord your God is the one who goes with you to fight for you against your enemies to give you victory (Deuteronomy 20:4).

Israel faced physical enemies they could see. These enemies were larger and better trained than the Israelites. God remained unconcerned. He prepared them for war by encouraging them with the statement that He "goes with you to fight." He trained the Israelites by teaching them to trust the One who gives victory. God declares victory for the believer before the battle even begins. He knows the result, and He asks us to remain focused on Him. Trust that God enters the battle and fights alongside His children. If He defeated death, hell, and the grave, He reigns victorious over the battles raging in our lives as well. Keep your eyes on Jesus during your battle. He wins every time.

Day 4 – Job 22:26-30 (MSG)

Watch your words

26-30 "You'll take delight in God, the Mighty One, and look to him joyfully, boldly. You'll pray to him and he'll listen; he'll help you do what you've promised. You'll decide what you want, and it will happen; your life will be bathed in light. To those who feel low you'll say, 'Chin up! Be brave!' and God will save them. Yes, even the guilty will escape, escape through God's grace in your life."

Just an Observation

"You will also declare a thing, and it will be established for you" Job 22:28 NKJV. It is not what others say to you or about you that determines your future; it's what you say to yourself after others get through talking! The Bible says, "Death and life are in the power of the tongue, and those who love it will eat its fruit" (Proverbs 18:21 NKJV). You say, "I would love to have a better relationship, but I'm afraid if I make the first move and they don't respond I'll feel rejected." Or "I would like to pursue my education, but I'm afraid if I register for classes and can't do the work, I'll feel stupid." Such words become self-fulfilling prophecies. Until you replace your negative self-talk with faith-talk you will always live-in fear. Our mind is like the womb of our spirit; it nurtures each seed we sow until the time of delivery. If you do not want what a seed will ultimately produce you must stop sowing it and feeding it. Your first step in breaking fear's hold over you, recognizing the self-talk that got you into trouble in the first place. Now, this is not easy to do. It takes vigilance, self-awareness, discipline, and scriptural reprogramming. However, by changing your thoughts you will begin to change your life. Job says, "You will…declare a thing, and it will be established for you." And the amazing part is, at times you may not feel like you believe the Scripture you are standing on. That is okay; your inner self accepts what it's consistently fed and begins to act accordingly. So, starting today, serve an eviction notice to every negative thought that's holding you back and begin feeding your mind with God's Word.

Day 5 - Philippians 3:7-9 (MSG)

The Cost of a Dream

7-9 The very credentials these people are waving around as something special, I'm tearing up and throwing out with the trash—along with everything else I used to take credit for. And why? Because of Christ. Yes, all the things I once thought were so important are gone from my life. Compared to the high privilege of knowing Christ Jesus as my Master, firsthand, everything I once thought I had going for me is insignificant—dog dung. I've dumped it all in the trash so that I could embrace Christ and be embraced by him. I didn't want some petty, inferior brand of righteousness that comes from keeping a list of rules when I could get the robust kind that comes from trusting Christ—God's righteousness.

Just an Observation

"I consider everything a loss…compared to…" Philippians 3:8 NIV. Your dream may not be fulfilled unless you are willing to pay the price that comes with it. And that price is paid not once, but over a lifetime. First, there is the initial cost. You will have to make personal and sometimes painful sacrifices. You may have to walk away from attractive options and valued relationships because they do not fit into God's plan for your life. Leaving things that have given you your security and your identity will require grit and grace that only God can provide. However, Paul's résumé included being "of the tribe of Benjamin, a Hebrew of the Hebrews…a Pharisee" (v. 5 NIV). Paul once had wealth and status. Paul's calling was to cover Asia with the gospel and write half of the New Testament. But great assignments call for great sacrifice. Paul was not alone. "By faith Moses, when he had grown up, refused to be known as the son of Pharaoh's daughter. He chose to be mistreated along with the people of God rather than to enjoy the pleasures of sin for a short time. He regarded disgrace for the sake of Christ as of greater value than the treasures of Egypt because he was looking ahead to his reward" (Hebrews 11:24-26 NIV). So, the question is: has God given you a dream? Do you have the faith and fortitude to fulfill it? Have you counted the cost and are you ready to pay it?

Day 6 – Proverbs 4:23-27 (MSG)

How is your Heart?

23-27 Keep vigilant watch over your heart; that's where life starts. Don't talk out of both sides of your mouth; avoid careless banter, white lies, and gossip. Keep your eyes straight ahead; ignore all sideshow distractions. Watch your step, and the road will stretch out smooth before you. Look neither right nor left; leave evil in the dust.

Just an Observation

"Above all…guard your heart…it is the wellspring of life" Proverbs 4:23 NIV. Heart disease will kill you if it's not detected and treated. Now, this is true both physically and spiritually. Therefore, the Bible says, "Above all…guard your heart, for it is the wellspring of life." Wanting to look our best is commendable. It can enhance our sense of self-worth and improve our prospects in life. But it is a big mistake to dwell on our appearance and neglect our character. When it's all said and done, "Man looks at the outward appearance, but the Lord looks at the heart" (1 Samuel 16:7 NIV). However, this is where the Bible comes into play. It's like a mirror; it shows you the condition of your heart at any given moment. With that being said, I have some questions to ask. How is your heart? What kind of thoughts are you entertaining? Are you constantly comparing and resenting? Do you get easily upset? When you hear gossip do you silence it or spread it? Jesus said, "Blessed are the pure in heart: for they shall see God" (Matthew 5:8 KJV). In other words when you start to see things God's way you will act accordingly. If the water in the well is polluted it will make you sick. Indeed, if you drink enough, it can kill you. What is the point? Glad you ask; simply this: it's not enough to try to change your bad habits; you've got to go to the heart of your problem—which is the problem of your heart! The Psalmist realized this, so he prayed, "Create in me a clean heart, O God; and renew a right spirit within me" (Psalm 51:10 KJV).

Day 7 – Galatians 6:9-10 (MSG)

God's Timing

9-10 So let's not allow ourselves to get fatigued doing good. At the right time we will harvest a good crop if we don't give up or quit. Right now, therefore, every time we get the chance, let us work for the benefit of all, starting with the people closest to us in the community of faith.

Just an Observation

"By your patience possess your souls" Luke 21:19 NKJV. When God makes us wait for something longer than we want to, He is teaching us patience. Our emotions are like a wild horse, they need to be reined in. "Patient endurance is what we need now, so that we will continue to do God will. Then we will receive all that he has promised" (Hebrew 10:36 NLT). Our impatience will just make us and everybody around us miserable, but it will not rush God. He works according to His own plan and timetable: "In due season we shall reap" (Galatians 6:9). "Due season" is God's season, not ours. We are in a hurry, He is not. He takes time to do things right. We may not know what He's doing, but He does; and that will have to be good enough for us. God's timing seems to be His own business; He's never late. He takes every opportunity to develop in us the fruit of patience. But other fruits are being developed in us as well. There are several things that must arrive at the finish line at the same time for us to win the race. Developed potential, without character, does not glorify God. If we were to become a huge success and yet be arrogant and harsh with people, that would not be pleasing to the Lord. So, when we get ahead of ourselves in one area, He gently but firmly blocks our progress in that area until the others catch up. We do not appreciate any of this while it's happening, but later we realize what a mess we would have made if things had been done on our timetable instead of Gods.

Day 8 – Deuteronomy 10:8-9 (MSG)

Speak Blessings

8-9 That's when GOD set apart the tribe of Levi to carry GOD's Covenant Chest, to be on duty in the Presence of GOD, to serve him, and to bless in his name, as they continue to do today. And that's why Levites don't have a piece of inherited land as their kinsmen do. GOD is their inheritance, as GOD, your God, promised them.

Just an Observation

Life's experiences can knock us down. How can we as believers help ourselves and others keep a Godly, positive outlook on life? Speak blessings to others. Words contain the power to uplift or tear down. Negative words can drive some to destructive choices. In contrast, positive words encourage others to great achievements. Words of blessing produce joy and hope. Knowing the impact of blessings, God gave the Levites the task of regularly blessing their fellow Israelites.

The Lord set apart the tribe of Levi to carry the ark of the covenant of the Lord, to stand before the Lord to minister and to pronounce blessings in His name (Deuteronomy 10:8). Today, the job of the Levites belongs to all believers, for Christians serve as God's priests (1 Peter 2:9). Therefore, the job of blessing others falls to all Christians. Blessings can be prayers spoken over another or declarations of God's goodness in a person's life.

Day 9 - 1 John 4:7-10 (MSG)

LOVE

7-10 My beloved friends, let us continue to love each other since love comes from God. Everyone who loves is born of God and experiences a relationship with God. The person who refuses to love doesn't know the first thing about God, because God is love—so you can't know him if you don't love. This is how God showed his love for us: God sent his only Son into the world so we might live through him. This is the kind of love we are talking about—not that we once upon a time loved God, but that he loved us and sent his Son as a sacrifice to clear away our sins and the damage they've done to our relationship with God.

Just an Observation

Love is slow to suspect but quick to trust; slow to condemn but quick to justify; slow to offend but quick to defend; slow to expose but quick to shield; slow to reprimand but quick to empathize; slow to belittle but quick to appreciate; slow to demand but quick to give; slow to provoke but quick to help; slow to resent but quick to forgive. Bestselling author Jerry Cook talks about a church where the people made the following pledge to each other: "I'll never knowingly say or do anything to hurt you. I'll always, in every circumstance, seek to help and support you. If you are down and I can lift you, I'll do that. If you need something and I have it, I will share it with you and if I need to, I'll give it to you. No matter what I find out about you, no matter what happens in the future—either good or bad—my commitment to you will never change. And there's nothing you can do about it." 1 Corinthians 13:7 NKJV says love: 1) "Believes all things." When someone you care about is called into question, love says, "That's not the kind of person they are; that's not what they meant." 2) "Hopes all things." Love sees people not just as they are, but as they can be through God's grace. And if you let Him, God will download that kind of love into your heart. 3) "Endures all things." The word "endure" is a military term. It means driving a stake into the ground. It's like saying, "I'll stand my ground in loving you." Today, take the love that God has given to you, and give it to others.

Day 10 – Hebrews 4:8-11 (MSG)

God Understands

8-11 And so this is still a live promise. It wasn't canceled at the time of Joshua; otherwise, God wouldn't keep renewing the appointment for "today." The promise of "arrival" and "rest" is still there for God's people. God himself is at rest. And at the end of the journey, we'll surely rest with God. So, let's keep at it and eventually arrive at the place of rest, not drop out through some sort of disobedience.

Just an Observation

The Lord understands what we are going through because He has been where we are. Scriptures states: "This High Priest of ours understands our weaknesses, for he faced all the same testing's we do…So let us come boldly to the throne of our gracious God. There we will receive mercy, and we will find grace to help us when we need it most" (vv.15-16 NLT). Now that means, Jesus understands our family problems. He had a family of His own. And on one occasion they said, "…He's out of His mind…" (Mark 3:21 NLT). Jesus understands when we feel overwhelmed. "Then Jesus said, "Let's go off by ourselves to a quiet place and rest awhile." He said this because there were so many people coming and going that Jesus and his apostles didn't even have time to eat." (Mark 6:31 NLT). Jesus not only dealt with on-the-job pressures, but He also had to organize, train, and correct His own followers, including a group of uneducated fishermen, a bigot, and a despised tax collector. Jesus understands when we feel rejected. The town He grew up in had no use for Him. "He came unto his own, and his own received him not" (John 1:11 KJV). In addition, Jesus family tree was nothing to write home about either. Rahab was a prostitute, Jacob was a crook, and David was an adulterer just to name a few. Oh Yes, Jesus understands. He knows where we are and He is able to help us. Just talk to Him!

Day 11 – Leviticus 26:12 (AMP)

Walking partner from heaven

And I will walk in and with and among you and will be your God, and you shall be My people.

Just an Observation

Go to the mall, a school, or a YMCA that has a place set aside for walking, and you will see it time and time again walking partners. You can get just as much physical benefit from the exercise of walking by doing it alone, but there is something special in having someone walk with you. In the last sentence in Matthew (28:20), we have another similar promise. Our Lord will walk with us always. Mile after mile, over smooth and rocky roads, up and down hills and mountains, and in sunshine and rain He will be there. We as walkers do not typically just keep track of the distance traveled but we discuss family and community issues. Most importantly we spend some of our time praying, knowing that we have the Walking Partner from heaven in our company. Go for a walk and enjoy talking to the Master it is a life changing experience.

Day 12 – James 4:4-6 (MSG)

Experiencing God Grace

4-6 You're cheating on God. If all you want is your own way, flirting with the world every chance you get, you end up enemies of God and his way. And do you suppose God doesn't care? The proverb has it that "he's a fiercely jealous lover." And what he gives in love is far better than anything else you'll find. Its common knowledge that "God goes against the willful proud; God gives grace to the willing humble."

Just an Observation

"Grace be unto you, and peace, from God" 1 Corinthians 1:3. Several of Paul's epistles open with the words, "Grace be unto you, and peace, from God." That is because you cannot experience God's peace unless you first know how to receive His grace and walk in it. There are three things about grace we need to understand: (a) it cannot be earned; (b) it is God doing for you, what you cannot do for yourself; (c) it does not kick in until you stop struggling and trying to do it in your own strength. The Bible says, "God opposes the proud but gives grace to the humble" (James 4:6 NIV). The "humble" are those who admit their total inability to succeed without God's help, but the "proud" are always trying to take credit. They like to think it's their ability that gets the job done, so they have difficulty asking God for grace, and even more difficulty receiving it. Peter writes, "Grow in grace" (2 Peter 3:18). You only learn to trust God—by doing it! You grow in grace by taking God at His Word, counting on His gracious provision for each day, and His intervention in situations that are difficult or impossible for you. There will never be a day when you do not need God's grace. And if you are willing to acknowledge you need it and receive it by faith, there will be no shortage of it. "For out of His fullness (abundance) we have all received [all had a share, and we were all supplied with] one grace after another and spiritual blessing upon spiritual blessing and even favor upon favor and gift [heaped] upon gift" (John 1:16 AMP).

Day 13 – Hebrews 13:5-6 (MSG)

GOD plus-----?

5-6 Don't be obsessed with getting more material things. Be relaxed with what you have. Since God assured us, "I'll never let you down, never walk off and leave you," we can boldly quote, God is there, ready to help; I'm fearless no matter what. Who or what can get to me?

Just an Observation

"Be content with such things as you have" Hebrews 13:5 NKJV. If our goals are God-centered, He will help us to achieve them. But if we are asking Him for something just because our neighbor has it, we will be disappointed. The Bible says, "No good thing will he withhold from them that walk uprightly" (Psalm 84:11). When God withholds something from us, trust Him; He knows what He is doing. God loves us too much to give us what we are not ready for, cannot handle, does not fit into His plan for our life, or will end up draining our energies and maybe even destroying us. When we covet something, make it essential to our happiness, and beg God to give it to us, we are asking God to replace Himself with something we consider more important. When we do this, God may allow us to experience the consequences Israel suffered. "He gave them their request; but sent leanness into their soul" (Psalm 106:15). Do not reach the end of your life only to look back with regret on a shattered marriage, children who have gone astray, a blighted conscience, or the pain of realizing you missed out on God's best. Our problem is not that we do not want God; it's that we want God—plus—a house by the lake, an impressive career, a perfect spouse, or whatever catches our fancy. That is why Jesus said, "Take heed and beware of covetousness, for one's life does not consist in the abundance of the things he possesses" (Luke 12:15 NKJV). Life is not built on things; it is built on relationships. And the first relationship you need to work on is your relationship with God.

Day 14 – 2 Timothy 1:5-7 (MSG)

Sound Thinking

5-7 That precious memory triggers another: your honest faith—and what a rich faith it is, handed down from your grandmother Lois to your mother Eunice, and now to you! And the special gift of ministry you received when I laid hands on you and prayed—keep that ablaze! God doesn't want us to be shy with his gifts, but bold and loving and sensible.

Just an Observation

"God has…given us…a sound mind" 2 Timothy 1:7 NKJV. The Bible says, "God has not given us a spirit of fear, but of power and of love and of a sound mind." I found out to improve my life I had to change two things: (1) My thought process. Author Gordon MacDonald says: "people who are out of shape mentally fall victim to ideas and systems that are destructive to the human spirit. They have not been taught how to think, nor have they set themselves to the life-long pursuit of the growth of the mind, so they grow dependent upon the thoughts and opinions of others. Rather than deal with ideas and issues, they reduce themselves to lives filled with rules, regulations and programs." The moment you think you know it all, you have merely stopped thinking. (2) My expectations. The story is told of a man who went to a fortuneteller. She said to him, "you'll be poor and miserable until you're fifty." The man asked her, "What will happen then?" She replied, "Then you'll get used to it". Faith produces excitement, commitment, energy, and characteristics that help you achieve success. If you would like to possess these qualities, then raise your expectation level and bring it into alignment with God's promises. "Whatever things you ask when you pray, believe that you receive them, and you will have them" (Mark 11:24 NKJV). Do you want to succeed where you have failed before? To become the person, you always hoped to be. Do not start by changing your actions, start by changing your mind. Renew it daily with God's Word. Nothing else you do will have as great an impact.

Day 15 – Ezekiel 37:9-14 (MSG)

Rejoicing in Trouble

9 He said to me, "Prophesy to the breath. Prophesy, son of man. Tell the breath, 'GOD, the Master, says, Come from the four winds. Come, breath. Breathe on these slain bodies. Breathe life!'"

10 So I prophesied, just as he commanded me. The breath entered them, and they came alive! They stood up on their feet, a huge army.

11 Then God said to me, "Son of man, these bones are the whole house of Israel. Listen to what they are saying: 'Our bones are dried up, our hope is gone, there's nothing left of us.'

12-14 "Therefore, prophesy. Tell them, 'GOD, the Master, says: I'll dig up your graves and bring you out alive—O my people! Then I will take you straight to the land of Israel. When I dig up graves and bring you out as my people, you will realize that I am GOD. I'll breathe my life into you, and you'll live. Then I will lead you straight back to your land and you'll realize that I am GOD. I have said it and I'll do it. GOD's Decree.'"

Just an Observation

"Breath came into them and they lived and stood upon their feet" Ezekiel 37:10 NKJV. Your hopes may be dead, and your dreams buried, but God can breathe into them again. Ezekiel stood in a valley of dead, dry bones. Then something amazing happened. God said to the Prophet, "Prophesy…and say…" Thus, says the Lord God: Come from the four winds, O breath, and breathe on these slain, that they may live." So, I prophesied as He commanded me, and breath came into them, and they lived, and stood upon their feet, an exceedingly great army" (vv. 9-10 NKJV). It was after he had been thrown out of the city, stoned and left for dead, that Paul spoke of being taken up into the third heaven and experiencing things too wonderful to speak of on earth (2 Corinthians 12:2-4). It was after John was exiled to a penal colony in Patmos that he penned the words, "I was in the Spirit, and I heard behind me a loud voice like a trumpet" (Revelation 1:10 NIV). As a result, he wrote the book of Revelation. The Psalmist said, "In the day of trouble …my head will be exalted above the enemies who surround me…I will sing…to the Lord" (Psalm 27:5-6 NIV). Now that is how you "glory in tribulation," then look back and be able to say, "Thank you for the experience, Lord. Without it I never would have gotten to know You like I do today."

Day 16 – Exodus 33:11 (MSG)

Friendship Privileges

And GOD spoke with Moses face-to-face, as neighbors speak to one another. When he would return to the camp, his attendant, the young man Joshua, stayed—he didn't leave the Tent.

Just an Observation

And GOD spoke with Moses face-to-face, as neighbors speak to one another. When he would return to the camp, his attendant, the young man Joshua, stayed—he did not leave the Tent. God communicated with Moses in ways He did not communicate with other Israelites. These face-to-face conversations frightened Moses fellow citizens. They saw the awesome power of God and did not see the personal side He offered to those who follow Him. Jesus declared in John 15:15 that His followers are no longer slaves but could now be called friends. That truth extends to everyone who serves the Lord today. He desires to be the best friend anyone could hope to have. He offers the privilege of His friendship to everyone who calls on Him as Lord and Savior. Lord, thank You for the privilege of being Your friend.

Day 17 – Exodus 28:41 (NKJV)

Job Opening

So, you shall put them on Aaron your brother and on his sons with him. You shall anoint them, consecrate them, and sanctify them, that they may minister to Me as priests.

Just an Observation

Imagine this in your local newspaper posting a job opening "Wanted": Someone who will serve Me, speak for Me, and shepherd My people. Perfection not required. Position cannot be earned. Applicants must be faithful to Me and walk-in obedience to My directions. Uniform provided. Interested? Call Me. God called Aaron and his sons to His service. Their assignment was important, and the clothing God directed had great meaning. They were washed, clothed, anointed, forgiven, dedicated, had the blood applied, served a meal, and given directions for ministry. Believers have been called to a holy priesthood (1Peter 2:9-10). God prepares us for this important job. We are washed in the cleansing blood, clothed in Christ's righteousness, anointed by the Spirit, forgiven by God's grace, covered by Christ's protecting blood, fed from His Word, and led by the Holy Spirit. Answer His call today. Ask God to prepare you daily for service to Him and His people.

Day 18 - Exodus 26:33 (Amplified Bible)

Limited Access

Read Exodus 25:1 through 27:21 And you shall hang the veil from the clasps and bring the ark of the Testimony into place within the veil; and the veil shall separate for you the Holy Place from the Most Holy Place.

Just an Observation

When the stage curtain is closed, it creates a separation between the performers and the audience. No one is to enter backstage. When closing a curtain to a window, the room becomes shaded. A curtain creates a barrier between people and things for a purpose. In the tabernacle, a curtain separated the Holy Place from the Most Holy Place. Only the high priest was to enter the Most Holy Place and then only on the Day of Atonement when he came in with the blood of the atoning sacrifice. This limited access into the presence of God was because of the sinful condition of the people. When Jesus died on the cross, the curtain was torn. Hebrews 10:19,20 states, "We have confidence to enter the Most Holy Place by the blood of Jesus, by a new and living way opened for us through the curtain, that is, his body." Jesus made the way for sinful people to enter the presence of the holy God—by making them holy. We have direct access to God. Is there a curtain keeping you from experiencing God's presence?

Day 19 – Exodus 14:22-25 (MSG)

God Fights for Us

Read Exodus 13:1 through 15:27 22-25 The Israelites walked through the sea on dry ground with the waters a wall to the right and to the left. The Egyptians came after them in full pursuit, every horse and chariot and driver of Pharaoh racing into the middle of the sea. It was now the morning watch. GOD looked down from the Pillar of Fire and Cloud on the Egyptian army and threw them into a panic. He clogged the wheels of their chariots; they were stuck in the mud. The Egyptians said, "Run from Israel! GOD is fighting on their side and against Egypt!"

Just an Observation

The Israelites went through the sea on dry ground, with a wall of water on their right and on their left (Exodus 14:22). The Israelites were leaving Egypt, being led by Moses, whom God had sent to deliver them from slavery. But now they were in a desperate situation. The Egyptian army was right behind them and the Red Sea was in front of them. They had no place to run or hide from the onslaught of their enemies. Fearful, they thought they were going to die. But God had a plan. He would rescue His people and bring glory to His name through the defeat of the Egyptians. God opened the Red Sea and the Israelites walked through on dry land. When the Egyptian army tried to follow them, they were drowned. The parting of the Red Sea should remind us of God's power and greatness and how He will fight for us. When God brings us through whatever crisis or issue, we face, let us give Him praise and glory. Remember, God fights for us. We can approach any situation with faith, knowing He can part the waters and lead us through victoriously. Lord, may I trust You through every situation.

Day 20 – Exodus 3:14 (NKJV)

Thank You Lord for ALWAYS being there

And God said to Moses, "I AM WHO I AM." And He said, thus you shall say to the children of Israel, 'I AM has sent me to you.

Just an Observation

Moses knew the Israelites would ask the name of the God who had sent him. So, he asked the Lord, "Who shall I say sent me?" God said to Moses, "I am who I am. This is what you are to say to the Israelites: 'I am has sent me to you' (Exodus 3:14). God's reply was interesting in that He did not really give a name. It was not the god of the sky or the god of the mountains. It was not the god of the past or the god of the future. In the simplest terms, God called himself "I AM"—the One who is present this very moment and is always nearby. God wanted the Children of Israel to know that He is always present, always existing, and ready to help them out of their bondage. Moses was going to represent a close and personal God. The God who was there to help Moses and Israel is available to help anyone today. He is a personal and caring God. He is still the "I am" and ready when called upon. Lord, thank You for always being there.

Day 21 - 2 Corinthians 12:7-10 (MSG)

I just let Christ take over!

7-10 Because of the extravagance of those revelations, and so I wouldn't get a big head, I was given the gift of a handicap to keep me in constant touch with my limitations. Satan's angel did his best to get me down; what he in fact did was push me to my knees. No danger then of walking around high and mighty! At first, I didn't think of it as a gift, and begged God to remove it. Three times I did that, and then he told me, My grace is enough; it's all you need. My strength comes into its own in your weakness. Once I heard that, I was glad to let it happen. I quit focusing on the handicap and began appreciating the gift. It was a case of Christ's strength moving in on my weakness. Now I take limitations in stride, and with good cheer, these limitations that cut me down to size—abuse, accidents, opposition, bad breaks. I just let Christ take over! And so, the weaker I get, the stronger I become.

Just an Observation

Speaking of his 'thorn', Paul writes: "I was given the gift of a handicap…At first I didn't think of it as a gift, and begged God to remove it…he told me, "My grace is enough; it is all you need. My strength comes into its own in your weakness." Once I heard that, I was glad to let it happen. I quit focusing on the handicap and began appreciating the gift…Now I take my limitations in stride, and with good cheer, these limitations that cut me down to size abuse, accidents, opposition, bad breaks. I just let Christ take over! And so, the weaker I get, the stronger I become" (vv. 7-10 The Message Bible). Paul learned how to turn his weakness into a weapon by allowing it to drive him closer to God. And that's a lesson I have learn too. "You're blessed when you're at the end of your rope. With less of you there is more of God and his rule" (see Matthew 5:3 The Message Bible). Now, you cannot just accept your character flaws and areas of defeat and say, "Well, I guess that's just the way I am." No, you must confront each area of weakness, confess it, and "let Christ take over". We will always struggle with one thing or another and Paul recognized this. "We carry this precious Message around in the unadorned clay pots of our ordinary lives. That's to prevent anyone from confusing God's incomparable power with us" (2 Corinthians 4:7 The Message Bible). Like common pottery, fragile, flawed and easily broken, God will use us as we surrender and allow Him to work through us.

Day 22 – Genesis 40:23 (MSG)

People will forget you; But God Does not

23 But the head cupbearer never gave Joseph another thought; he forgot all about him.

Just an Observation

Joseph had lived through some of the worst experiences a person could imagine. Sold into slavery by his brothers, falsely accused of attempted rape, and thrown into prison. How many injustices could one person take? Finally, Joseph was promised help from a fellow cellmate after Joseph had helped him. The chief cupbearer, however, did not remember Joseph; he forgot him (Genesis 40:23). I can imagine what went through Joseph's mind. He may have thought that was his last chance to get out of prison. But eventually the cupbearer remembered Joseph. God revealed Pharaoh's dream to Joseph, and he was released and rose to a powerful position. A position the Lord used to save his family and the line of Christ. I do not know about you, but I have suffered many injustices and even been forgotten by friends and family. It can be frustrating and leave you feeling hopeless, used, and taken advantage of. But just like the Lord remembered Joseph, He knows our situation. He loves us and He intends good for everything He allows into our life, whether we understand it or not. We are never forgotten. God has a perfect memory, and our name is in His book.

Day 23 – John 11:40 (MSG)

Is there anything too hard for God?

40 Jesus looked her in the eye. "Didn't I tell you that if you believed, you would see the glory of God?"

Just an Observation

"If you would believe you would see the glory of God." (John 11:40 NKJV) In the story of Jesus raising Lazarus from the dead I notice three important principles. The first one is Mary and Martha had a close relationship with Jesus before the crisis arose. When Jesus came to town He stayed at their home and ate at their table. They were givers, not takers. You cannot refuse to give God a minute of your time, an ounce of your energy, or a penny of your money, then when trouble comes, say, "Lord, why did You let this happen?" Jesus said, "If you abide in Me, and My words abide in you, you will ask what you desire, and it shall be done for you" (John 15:7 NKJV). The second principle I notice is having a relationship with Jesus does not mean you will not have trouble. But it does mean that you can go to Him with confidence in times of trouble. Yes, we must pay attention to our career and family, but we must also pay attention to the most important relationship of all; the one we have with the Lord. "If our hearts do not condemn us, we have confidence before God and receive from him anything we ask, because we obey his commands and do what pleases him" (1John 3:21-22 NIV). The last value I am a witness to is when you bring Jesus into the situation, He will change it. Scripture reveals Lazarus was already dead and buried by the time Jesus got there. Realistically speaking, it was a hopeless situation. But in moments like these God asks us, "Is there anything too hard for me?" (Jeremiah 32:27). If your answer is "No, Lord," then your problem becomes an opportunity for Him to demonstrate His love and care for you.

Day 24 – Genesis 30:6-8 (MSG)

Be Patient, Not Jealous!

6-8 Rachel said, "God took my side and vindicated me. He listened to me and gave me a son." She named him Dan (Vindication). Rachel's maid Bilhah became pregnant again and gave Jacob a second son. Rachel said, "I've been in an all-out fight with my sister—and I've won." So, she named him Naphtali (Fight).

Just an Observation

Leah and Rachel were jealous of each other. Rachel had Jacob's love, but she was barren. Leah was not loved by Jacob, but she was able to bear him sons. This created a great rivalry between the sisters. It must have been hard for two sisters to be married to the same man, and they did not handle it well. Instead of praying to God to meet their needs and desires, they took matters into their own hands. They gave their servant girls to Jacob to bear more children. The servants conceived, but despite their blessings, the jealous hatred between the sisters continued.

God does work through sinful people. He blessed the families as He had promised. But the rivalry between Leah and Rachel caused a lot of strife within the family. There was division among their sons for many years. How might the story of Jacob's family have been different had they simply been patient with each other and trusted God? Help me, God, to wait on You. Forgive my discontent. Thank You for Your blessings.

Day 25 – Matthew 5:10 (MSG)

In the Fire

10 "You're blessed when your commitment to God provokes persecution. The persecution drives you even deeper into God's kingdom.

Just an Observation

"Blessed are those who are persecuted for righteousness' sake" Matthew 5:10 NKJV. In Yellowstone National Park there is an interesting tree called a Lodgepole Pine. Its cones can hang on for years before falling off and even then, they remain tightly closed. They open only when they are in contact with intense heat. Whenever forest fires are raging and all the trees are being destroyed, the heat opens these pinecones. As a result, they are the first to assist nature in repopulating the forest. Jesus said to His disciples, "Blessed are those who are persecuted for righteousness' sake, for theirs is the kingdom of heaven." There's potential in each of us that is only released when we're under pressure or in a fiery trial. Job discovered this when God permitted Satan to test him. Job lost everything he had, including his children. And to add insult to injury, he was forced to endure the scorn of his wife and friends because of his unwavering faith. When it was over, Job, who got back twice as much as he lost, prayed, "I have heard of You by the hearing of the ear, but now my eye sees You" (Job 42:5 NKJV). It's one thing to hear how God works based on someone else experience, it's another to see it first-hand in your own life. I have learned through personal experiences it's in the fire that I discover new aspects of God's care and character. I also learned what turns worthless carbon into diamonds is Heat and Pressure! The most important thing, while in the fire I discovered, when everyone abandoned me God remained faithful and is still faithful. Jesus is a friend and will never ever leave you; trust me I know this personally.

Day 26 – Genesis 22:14 (NKJV)

God Will Provide

14 And Abraham called the name of the place, The-LORD-Will-Provide; as it is said to this day, "In the Mount of the LORD it shall be provided."

Just an Observation

Blessing comes from obedience to God. In Genesis 22, God tested Abraham by asking him to make the ultimate sacrifice his son. As difficult as it must have been for Abraham, he was willing to kill his son on the altar because God had asked him to. At the last minute, because of Abraham's obedience, God provided a ram for Abraham to sacrifice instead of his son Isaac. Abraham had faith that God would provide. God had promised to bless Abraham and make his descendants numerous and great. Abraham trusted in that promise. He was willing to sacrifice his son, and he was rewarded for his obedience. God provides for our needs. When Abraham needed a place to bury his wife, Sarah, the cave in the field of Machpelah was provided. When Abraham needed to find a wife from his own country for his son Isaac, Rebekah was provided. The Scriptures are full of examples of God's provision for our needs when we trust and obey His will for our lives. Always obey God and hold to His promises.

Day 27 – Matthew 5:5 (MSG)

Meekness

5 "You're blessed when you're content with just who you are—no more, no less. That's the moment you find yourselves proud owners of everything that can't be bought.

Just an Observation

In our macho world, meekness is often mistaken for weakness. But Jesus definition of meekness pictures a powerful, majestic stallion that has been brought into submission. It has not lost any of its stamina; it is just that, whereas it once had a strong will of its own, it now yields to the will of another. The breaking process is complete; now it responds to the tug on the reins. Meekness involves being Sensitivity to God and Surrender to God's will. The key to breaking stubborn habits is not fighting them in your own strength; that only keeps your focus on the problem, intensifying its power. Changing your focus and submitting to God moment by moment is the key to winning, whether it is a problem or a hang-up. "Not that we are sufficient of ourselves to think of anything as being from ourselves, but our sufficiency is from God" (2 Corinthians 3:5 NKJV) Meekness also involves Submission to God's purposes. To understand the difference between submission and selfishness ponder on these words from Ezekiel 33:31, "So they come to you as people do, they sit before you as My people, and they hear your words, but they do not do them; for with their mouth, they show much love, but their hearts pursue their own gain."

Day 28 – Proverbs 13:4 (MSG)

The Extra Step

Indolence wants it all and gets nothing; the energetic have something to show for their lives.

Just an Observation

The sluggard craves and gets nothing, but the desires of the diligent are fully satisfied." Proverbs 13:4 NIV the word "diligence" includes such qualities as hard work, honesty, persistence, and striving for excellence. The New Living Bible Translation puts it this way: "Lazy people want much but get little, but those who work hard will prosper." Another expert says, "Success doesn't come from being a hundred percent better than your competition, but from being one percent better in a hundred different ways." Syndicated business columnist Dale Dauten says: "If you want to be creative in your company, your career or your life, it all comes down to one easy step…the extra one. When you encounter a familiar plan, you just ask one question: 'What else could we do?'" To succeed you will have to do more— more than you may want, more than your competition, more than you think you're capable of. The poet William Arthur Ward said: "I will do more than belong—I will participate. I will do more than care—I will help. I will do more than believe—I will practice. I will do more than be fair—I will be kind. I will do more than forgive—I will forget. I will do more than dream—I will work. I will do more than teach—I will inspire. I will do more than learn—I will enrich. I will do more than give—I will serve. I will do more than live—I will grow. I will do more than suffer—I will triumph." You can't do whatever's easiest and still reach your goal. You must do more. You must do "whatever it takes.

Day 29 – Esther 4:15-16 (GNT)

You Can Do IT!

15 Esther sent Mordecai this reply: 16 "Go and get all the Jews in Susa together; hold a fast and pray for me. Don't eat or drink anything for three days and nights. My servant women and I will be doing the same. After that, I will go to the king, even though it is against the law. If I must die for doing it, I will die."

Just an Observation

Esther, a Jewish girl married to a pagan king, broke with long-standing tradition, marched into her husband's throne room, spoke her mind, and rescued her people from annihilation. One girl saved a nation because she was willing to put everything on the line. Are you feeling inadequate today? Are you thinking, 'Someone else should be doing this job instead of me'? Read these words written by clergyman Edward Everett Hale: 'I am only one; but still, I am one. I can't do everything; but still, I can do something: and because I can't do everything, I will not refuse to do the something I can do.' How many people did it take to rescue the dying man on the Jericho Road? One Good Samaritan! How many people did it take to confront Pharaoh and lead the exodus out of Egypt? One man, Moses! A respected leadership expert writes: 'God has put a dream inside you. It is yours and no one else. It declares your uniqueness. It holds your potential. Only you can give birth to it. Only you can live it. Not to discover it, take responsibility for it and act upon it is to negatively affect yourself as well as all those who would benefit from your dream.' Poet John Greenleaf Whittier wrote, 'For all sad words of tongue and pen; the saddest are these, "It might have been."' In your twilight years, will you look back and feel like you have spent your life struggling to fulfill other people's expectations? Or know that you lived it to the fullest by striving to fulfill your God-given dream?

Day 30 – Hebrews 11:1 (GNT)

"NOW" Faith

To have faith is to be sure of the things we hope for, to be certain of the things we cannot see.

Just an Observation

When you are in the middle of a crisis, what you really believe manifests itself in your words, attitude and actions. When Lazarus died and his sister Martha said, 'Lord, if you had been here, my brother would not have died' (John 11:21 NCV), she was voicing past-tense faith. When Jesus said, '[Lazarus] will…live again' (v 23 NCV) and she replied, 'I know that he will…live…in the resurrection…' (v 24 NCV), that was future-tense faith. And when she said, '…Even now God will give you anything you ask' (v 22 NCV), she was demonstrating 'now' faith, which is present tense. As believers, the Bible tells us not to '…look at the things which are seen, but at the things which are not seen…' (2 Corinthians 4:18 NKJV). 'Now' faith stakes its claim on 'something…even if we do not see it' (Hebrews 11:1 NCV). Paul says, '…we walk by faith, not by sight' (2 Corinthians 5:7 NKJV). Too often we base our feelings on what we see, instead of what God says in His Word. But as the author Jon Walker writes: 'When we believe that reality is confined to what we see, we become trapped into thinking the only truth is what we see. We become prisoners of our own perceptions; we cease walking in faith…For those who walk by faith, appearances are never the ultimate reality…Reality extends beyond what you can see…the things we do not see are eternal [time and circumstance do not diminish or alter them] (2 Corinthians 4:18 NIV). Even though things may appear bad, God is working things out for our good (Romans 8:28). He knows how the story ends, so fix your eyes on the unseen and not on what you see.'

Day 31 – John 3:16 (GNT)

Jesus loves me! This I know, for the Bible tells me so.

16 For God loved the world so much that he gave his only Son, so that everyone who believes in him may not die but have eternal life.

Just an Observation

David said, 'Blessed is he whose transgression is forgiven, whose sin is covered' (Psalms 32:1 NKJV). No matter how hard we worked, we could never pay off our sin debt. And thank God we do not have to, because 'God so loved the world, that He gave His only begotten Son, that whosoever believeth in Him should not perish, but have everlasting life.' Years ago, a congregation decided to honor one of its retired pastors. He was ninety-two, and some people wondered why the church even asked the elderly man to speak. After a warm welcome and introduction, he rose from his chair and walked with great dignity and effort to the pulpit. Leaning on the podium to steady himself, without notes of any kind, he began to speak: 'When your pastor invited me here, he asked me to talk about the greatest lesson I've learned in fifty-plus years of preaching. I have thought about it for a few days and boiled it down to the one thing that has made the most difference in my life and sustained me through all my trials. The one thing I can rely on when tears, heartbreak, pain, fear, and sorrow paralyze me…the one thing that always comforts me: Jesus loves me! This I know, for the Bible tells me so. Little ones to Him belong. They are weak but He is strong. Yes, Jesus loves me. Yes, Jesus loves me. Yes, Jesus loves me. The Bible tells me so.' You could hear a pin drop as the old man shuffled back to his seat. It is something the congregation never forgot. And it is something you should never forget either—Jesus loves you unconditionally. That is so today, tomorrow, and forever!

Day 32 – 2 Corinthians 9:8-11 (GNT)

And God Shall Supply

8 And God is able to give you more than you need, so that you will always have all you need for yourselves and more than enough for every good cause. 9 As the scripture says,

"He gives generously to the needy;

   his kindness lasts forever."

10 And God, who supplies seed for the sower and bread to eat, will also supply you with all the seed you need and will make it grow and produce a rich harvest from your generosity.

11 He will always make you rich enough to be generous at all times, so that many will thank God for your gifts which they receive from us.

Just an Observation

…God shall supply all your need according to His riches in glory' (Philippians 4:19 NKJV). Whose riches? God's! And His ability to bless you is not limited by the job market, the stock market, or the housing market. For forty years He fed His people in the wilderness with manna from heaven. He sent ravens to deliver meat to Elijah during a famine. He fed five thousand people with a boy's lunch. Paul writes, 'God will generously provide all you need. Then you will always have everything you need, and plenty left over to share with others…Yes, you will be enriched in every way…' (2 Corinthians 9:8, 11 NLT). The scarcity attitude is rooted in fear and shows distrust of the awesome power of God to supply all our needs according to His unlimited resources. It's based upon the faulty assumption that if someone else has something, you can't have it because there's only one pie, and every slice that someone else gets means less is available for you. It makes you believe that the blessings of others come at your expense. It says, 'You win, I lose.' That's no way to live the abundant life! Start today to reprogram your thinking. Remind yourself that you're not in competition with anybody, for anything, in any area of your life. Cling to the words of Jesus: '…I have come that [you] may have life, and that [you] may have it more abundantly' (John 10:10 NKJV). Pray: 'Father, help me to reject all thoughts of scarcity. Show me how to help others achieve their goals by sharing my time, talents, treasure. In Jesus' name, I pray. Amen.'

Day 33 – Proverbs 27:12 (ASV)

Cables

12 A prudent man seeth the evil, and hideth himself; But the simple pass on, and suffer for it.

Just an Observation

Half Dome is a granite peak that towers above the valley floor in Yosemite National Park. Your final climb is between steel cables bolted to the rock; they were designed as handholds to safeguard and help you reach the top. Columnist Mary Hunt writes: 'The final ascent up the sheer granite surface…is by far the most challenging. Once you see the cables you experience terror like you've never known…and you've no choice but to finish the trip. At that moment you're thankful for cables that become the guardrails you need to pull yourself to the top. The secret to [continuing] when you feel like quitting is to erect 'cables' in your life before you need them so that when you face difficult situations, the help you need to make it will be there to protect you from your own fears and self-defeating attitudes.' Solomon says, 'A prudent person foresees danger and takes precautions. The simpleton goes blindly on and suffers the consequences.' Sooner or later, you'll face a mountain you can't conquer alone. And if the 'cables' you need are in place, you'll conquer it. What are they? (1) God's Word. Jeremiah said, 'Your words…sustain me' (Jeremiah 15:16 TLB). Get into God's Word and get God's Word into you. That way, when trouble comes, you'll be able to handle it. It'll '…guide you when you walk…guard you when you sleep…speak to you when you are awake' (Proverbs 6:22 NCV). (2) A strong prayer life. '…The prayer of a person living right with God is something powerful to be reckoned with' (James 5:16 TM). Time spent with God changes you; it makes you more like Jesus and strengthens you for what lies ahead.

Day 34 – Acts 5:29 (GNT)

Set yourself "Free" from pleasing people

29 Peter and the other apostles answered, "We must obey God, not men.

Just an Observation

Too often our actions are dictated by a misguided need to please others. We care so much about what they think that with every step we take we look over our shoulder to see whether they're smiling or frowning. Understand this; if you're always looking for people's approval, you're not looking where you're going and eventually, you'll hit a wall or trip over your own two feet. The Bible says, '…We ought to obey God rather than men.' What do you think will happen if you open your mouth and stand up for yourself? The truth is that people who don't respect your rights and honor your wishes are not worth your time or effort. Nor are they worthy of a long-drawn-out discussion; just say goodbye! (We're not talking about your marriage or children.) When the land became too small for the flocks of Abraham and Lot to graze together, strife broke out. Abraham loved his nephew Lot, but he realized he could no longer live in this situation. So, he said, '…Please separate from me. If you take the left, then I will go to the right; or, if you go to the right, then I will go to the left' (Genesis 13:9 NKJV). How does their story end? Lot chose the best grazing land close to Sodom, and as a result everything he worked for went up in smoke. But Abraham, who always sought to please God, ended up not only being blessed himself, but being a blessing to the nations of the world. So, the word for us today is—God wants to set us free from people pleasing.

Day 35 – Deuteronomy 29:29 (GNT)

When We Don't Understand

29 "There are some things that the Lord our God has kept secret; but he has revealed his Law, and we and our descendants are to obey it forever.

Just an Observation

When you do not understand what is happening in your life, start with what you know for sure; namely, that God is good all the time, and His '…love for those who respect him continues forever…' (Psalms 103:17 NCV). He is not fickle. He does not bless you one day and curse you the next: His 'mercies…are new every morning' (Lamentations 3:22-23). But there are things God chooses to reveal to us, and 'secret things' He doesn't—for our own good. Writer Beth Jones says: 'If God keeps a secret from us, it's for our benefit and the benefit of others …For example, He doesn't go around blaming, tattling, or disclosing our sins, weaknesses, unbelief, carnality, selfishness or pride to others. When things happen, God knows why…Secret things belong to the Lord. And when He reveals something to us, it is because He wants us to walk in that truth by faith. For example, He reveals His character and His will in His Word…so we can live by faith knowing that He is good, fair, kind, generous, merciful, faithful, gracious, patient, and He is in the saving, healing, redeeming, restoring, sanctifying, and blessing business. Things revealed belong to us. When we do not know why …here is what we know for sure. God's Word is truer than our circumstances or experiences…and just because He knows everything about us does not mean He tells us about everything. We also know that when things look bad, God is still good. He's a giver, not a taker…a blesser, not a curser…and no matter what happens or doesn't happen, at the end of the day—we still win!'

Day 36 – Psalm 62:8 (GNT)

PRAY AND KEEP PRAYING

Trust in God at all times, my people.
   Tell him all your troubles,
   for he is our refuge.

Just an Observation

More than anything else in life, Hannah wanted a son. And as the years passed, she wrestled with disappointment and despair. '…in bitterness of soul (Hannah) wept much and prayed to the Lord' (1 Samuel 1:10 (NKJV). However, she did two things that worked—and they'll work for you, too! (1) Instead of turning away from God, she turned to Him. Instead of praying less, she prayed more. She knew that while her husband couldn't give her a child, God could. She may not have been happy with God's timing, but she never doubted His goodness. Unfortunately, one of the things we're tempted to do when things fall apart is to avoid God's presence. That's a mistake, because He's the one you need most! Yes, it's hard to pray when your heart is breaking. But unless you've prayed with a broken heart and a deep sense of your need, you've never really poured out your heart before God, or learned what the Bible truly means by prayer. (2) She didn't just think about what she wanted, she also thought about what God wanted. '…she made a vow, saying, "Lord Almighty, if you will…not forget your servant but give her a son, then I will give him to the Lord for all the days of his life…"' (v 11 NIV). And shortly after that Samuel was conceived. When you're willing to make a promise to God that He can hold you to (which is what a vow is), you're getting serious about prayer. And that's when God will get serious about your prayer as well! So, 'pour out your heart before Him'.

Day 37 – Proverbs 17:9 (GNT)

Forgive and move on

9 If you want people to like you, forgive them when they wrong you. Remembering wrongs can break up a friendship.

Just an Observation

Countless friendships and family relationships are destroyed because one person gets offended by something the other one said or did. A mark of spiritual growth is how quickly you get over slights and insults; the more mature you are, the less time it takes to 'forgive an offense' and move on. One Christian writer says: 'Okay, your friend ditches you and your feelings are hurt…or they're too busy to return your phone call or email… Offenses come…Jesus said they would (John 16:33). People are people. If you've been offended by a friend or family member, or felt slighted, get over it! Hit the Control>Alt>Delete buttons. Do not let bitterness even think about putting down roots…"Love…is not irritable…it keeps no record of being wronged…never gives up…and endures through every circumstance" (1 Corinthians 13:4-7 NLT). It seems impossible…and without God's love it is. So, yield to His love, overlook offenses and walk-in love, because next week you might be the one needing unconditional love. When it comes to being perfect, we have all failed. If we want our friends and family to overlook our offenses, be quick to overlook theirs.' Make this your prayer today: 'Father, thank You for the relationships You've blessed me with. I decide today to release anyone who has ever offended me in the slightest…to overlook it… forget about it and move on. I will not keep a record of their wrongs. I will offer mercy and unconditional love. In Jesus' name. Amen.'

Day 38 – Psalm 78:52 (GNT)

What we need in the Wilderness – Day 1

52 Then he led his people out like a shepherd
 and guided them through the desert.

Just an Observation

'My Lord knows the way through the wilderness; all I have to do is follow.' To get them from Egypt to Canaan, God took His people through the wilderness and, spiritually speaking; we will have to go through it, too! You can have a wilderness experience anywhere. At a grave-side, in a cancer ward, in a divorce court and in the unemployment line. But the wilderness can also be a place of miracles. So, this week, let us look at some things we need to survive in the wilderness. Direction is the first thing that comes to mind! Without it we end up going around in circles. Notice how God led Israel. He 'went before them by day in a pillar of a cloud…and by night in a pillar of fire, to give them light…He took not away the pillar of the cloud…nor the pillar of fire…from before the people' (Exodus 13:21-22 NKJV). God told Moses: 'Whenever the pillar moves, you move. And when the pillar stops, you stop.' But what do you do at night when it is pitched black? There are no candles or oil lamps, and you risk sharing your bed with a scorpion or stepping on a snake on your way to the bathroom. Don't worry; God's got you covered! The wilderness is not alien territory to Him. The Psalmist said, 'Your Word is a lamp to my feet and a light to my path' (Psalms 119:105 NKJV). For every contingency, condition, and circumstance we face, our Bible will guide us, protect us, and keep us safe. So, stop worrying and start reading it every day.

Day 39 – Psalm 78:53-54 (GNT)

What we need in the Wilderness – Day 2 (Food)

53 He led them safely, and they were not afraid;
    but the sea came rolling over their enemies.
54 He brought them to his holy land,
    to the mountains which he himself conquered.

Just an Observation

You can be in the wilderness and still be in the center of God's will. '…He made His own people go forth like sheep and guided them in the wilderness like a flock…He led them on safely, so…they did not fear…' (vv 52-53 NKJV). In the wilderness you get to know God in a way you never knew Him before. So, what else did Israel need to survive in the wilderness? Food! Someone calculated it would have taken about twenty-six wagonloads of food to feed that many Israelites every day. The problem is there were no trains and no tracks! But they had something much better—God! For forty years He delivered manna, 'the perfect food', to the doors of their tents. The supply was according to each family's individual need and God never missed a day. So, if the economy has you feeling anxious and wondering whether God can take care of you this is the word for you today! God may not give you everything you want, but He will give you everything you need. The God we serve does not suffer from lack or limitation! The Psalmist said, 'I have been young, and now am old; yet I have not seen the righteous forsaken, nor his descendants begging for bread' (Psalms 37:25 NKJV). 'Where He leads me, I will follow; what He feeds me I will swallow.' Think of it: for forty years Israel never missed a meal or went without, so put your trust in Him today and stop worrying!

Day 40 - Deuteronomy 8:15-18 (GNT)

What we need in the Wilderness – Day 3 (Water)

15 He led you through that vast and terrifying desert where there were poisonous snakes and scorpions. In that dry and waterless land, he made water flow out of solid rock for you. 16 In the desert he gave you manna to eat, food that your ancestors had never eaten. He sent hardships on you to test you, so that in the end he could bless you with good things. 17 So then, you must never think that you have made yourselves wealthy by your own power and strength. 18 Remember that it is the Lord your God who gives you the power to become rich.

Just an Observation

What else do you need in the wilderness? Water! You can live without food for about forty days, but without water you'll die much faster. It's the same in the spiritual realm; you can get by in life without a lot of things, but you won't make it without God. In the wilderness God was teaching His people a lesson He wanted them to remember when they arrived in the Promised Land: 'Otherwise, when you eat and are satisfied, when you build fine houses and settle down, and when your herds and flocks grow large and your silver and gold increase and all you have is multiplied, then your heart will become proud and you will forget the Lord…Who brought you out of…slavery. He led you through the vast and dreadful wilderness, that thirsty and waterless land, with its venomous snakes and scorpions. He brought you water out of hard rock. He gave you manna to eat in the wilderness, something your ancestors had never known, to humble and to test you so that in the end it might go well with you' (vv 12-16 NIV). Note the words 'that it might go well with you'. Despite what you're going through today, God has great blessings in store for you. But in order to handle them properly you must learn humility, develop a heart of gratitude, and never forget that He alone is the source of every good thing you'll ever have.

Day 41 – Psalm 105:37 (GNT)

What we need in the Wilderness – Day 4 (Divine Health)

37 Then he led the Israelites out;

   they carried silver and gold,

   and all of them were healthy and strong.

Just an Observation

Notice something else Israel enjoyed in the wilderness: divine health. Think of the health issues you'd expect among two million people walking through endless desert with no doctor or hospital in sight. Yet from the youngest to the oldest, 'He…brought them out…and there was none feeble among His tribes.' That is because they lived on a diet provided by God Himself. Their troubles began when they complained and wanted to go back to the food they ate as slaves in Egypt. Hello! There is an important lesson here for those who live on fast foods that promote ailments like heart disease, cancer, and diabetes. Imagine pouring five pounds of sugar into the fuel tank of your car and complaining that it won't run properly. Now, when health problems run in your family, or economic circumstances force you to eat less than ideal food, God understands and you can go to Him with confidence, believing, '…the prayer of faith will save the sick, and the Lord will raise him up…' (James 5:15 NKJV). But when the choice is between exercising wisdom to have good health or exercising faith in order to be healed, your choice is clear. When Israel entered the Promised Land, God told them, '…serve the Lord…and He will bless your bread and your water…take sickness away from the midst of you…[and] fulfill the number of your days' (Exodus 23:25-26 NKJV). Then He gave them dietary laws to live by that set them apart from the surrounding nations. Question: How many of us fail to 'fulfill the number of [our] days' and the assignment God gives us, because we refuse to exercise discipline when it comes to our diet? Think about it!

Day 42 – Job 22:21 (GNT)

What we need in the Wilderness – Day 5 (God)

Now, Job, make peace with God
 and stop treating him like an enemy;
 if you do, then he will bless you.

Just an Observation

When you find yourself in the wilderness, what's the one thing you need more than anything else? God! That's why the Lord told Moses to build the tabernacle and He used it as a teaching tool to show His people that: (1) He wants to meet with us regularly. The word 'tabernacle' means 'tent of meeting'. God wants us to spend time with Him. He wants you to get to know Him. Because when you do, you'll worry less and trust Him more. The Bible says, 'Acquaint now thyself with Him, and be at peace…' It's important to listen to God's Word being taught, to meet with other believers, and be encouraged by their testimonies. But at some point, we've got to stop trading in second-hand information and get 'up close and personal' with God. James writes, 'Draw near to God and He will draw near to you' (James 4:8 NKJV). (2) God wants to be at the center of our lives. When Israel set up camp each night, the twelve tribes pitched their tents in formation surrounding the tabernacle, where God's presence dwelt. Every man, woman, boy and girl could stand in the door of their tent and see God in their midst. Could the message be clearer? When our deepest affections and greatest ambitions are centered on Christ, our life will take an upward swing. '…delight yourself in the Lord and He will give you the desires of your heart' (Psalms 37:4 NIV). The formula for thriving in the wilderness is to center our life on Christ and soak ourselves in His Word!

Day 43 – Psalm 23:3 (GNT)

Take care of yourself

He gives me new strength.
He guides me in the right paths,
   as he has promised.

Just an Observation

David said, 'The Lord is my shepherd; I shall not want. He makes me to lie down in green pastures; He leads me beside the still waters. He restores my soul…' (vv 1-3 NKJV). Today car engines are computerized. A light on your dashboard will let you know something is wrong and that it's time for a checkup. Your soul will do that too. But you've got to pay attention to the signals! Do not wait until you have a spiritual, moral, emotional or relational breakdown before you stop and pay attention. When your soul's thirst is not quenched and its needs are not met, it will seek relief some other way, often a way that will hurt you. You must know when to say 'when'. Most of us don't take breaks that enable us to 'restore our souls'. We're ensnared by guilt, as if stopping would somehow be irresponsible. Or we fear losing ground because we took a minute for ourselves. One of the hardest things in life to achieve is not success, but a sense of balance. So, in all your goal setting and 'go-getting', don't forget your soul. Even God rested (Genesis 2:2). And if He did, then you need to also. The power of rest is that it allows you to enjoy the journey of life and not just the destination. Indeed, if you don't learn to walk in the park by choice, you may end up in the hospital by necessity. So, when God 'makes you lie down in green pastures', enjoy them, when He 'leads you beside the still waters', it's to refresh and restore you. So, practice soul care!

Day 44 – Job 1:9-12 (GNT)

A Wall of Protection

9 Satan replied, "Would Job worship you if he got nothing out of it? 10 You have always protected him and his family and everything he owns. You bless everything he does, and you have given him enough cattle to fill the whole country. 11 But now suppose you take away everything he has—he will curse you to your face!"
12 "All right," the Lord said to Satan, "everything he has is in your power, but you must not hurt Job himself." So, Satan left.

Just an Observation

When God praised Job for his integrity, Satan replied, 'You have always put a wall of protection around him…take away everything he has, and he will surely curse you.' So, God gave Satan permission to test Job, but He placed limits on how far he could go (Job 2:6). There are times '…When the enemy comes in like a flood' (Isaiah 59:19 NKJV) to attack your mind, your marriage, your ministry, and anything that's born of God in your life. When that happens, Isaiah says, '…The Spirit of the Lord will lift up a standard [shield] against him' (Isaiah 59:19 NKJV). When you feel you're at breaking point and can't handle one more thing, the Holy Spirit lifts the wall of the blood of Jesus and tells Satan, 'This far and no further!' Paul says, 'We are hard pressed on every side, but not crushed; perplexed, but not in despair; persecuted, but not abandoned; struck down, but not destroyed' (2 Corinthians 4:8-9 NIV). There's a wall of protection around you. There's also a time for your deliverance. '…In the time of my favor I heard you, and in the day of salvation I helped you' (2 Corinthians 6:2 NIV). God will step in and intervene. The Psalmist said, '…When my heart is faint; Lead me to the rock that is higher than I' (Psalm 61:2 NAS). When your resources are depleted and you think you're going under for the last time, God has provided a refuge that's higher than your circumstances, a place where you're under divine protection and the enemy has no jurisdiction. All you must do is lift your eyes toward heaven.

Day 45 – Matthew 6:31-34 (GNT)
Struggling? (God already know your needs!)

31 "Therefore do not worry, saying, 'What shall we eat?' or 'What shall we drink?' or 'What shall we wear?' 32 For after all these things the Gentiles seek. **For your heavenly Father knows** that you need all these things. 33 But seek first the kingdom of God and His righteousness, and all these things shall be added to you. 34 Therefore do not worry about tomorrow, for tomorrow will worry about its own things. Sufficient for the day is its own trouble.

Just an Observation

I have learned to replace panic with peace by praying for: (1) Clarity - Money is linked to our self-esteem. It can trigger feelings of shame, fear, pride, and anger. But "understanding [God's] Word brings light to the minds of ordinary people" (Psalms 119:130 CEV). (2) Creativity - If you want more money, you must earn more or spend less. We serve a creative God, and He rewards those who "…diligently seek him" (Hebrews 11:6 NKJV). Ask Him to show you how to increase your income. (3) Connections - kids are familiar with connect-the-dot puzzles, where you join a random collection of dots to produce an image you'd otherwise miss. It is all about the right connections, and God can send the right people into your life with answers to your money problems. (4) Contentment - just like earthquakes expose structural weaknesses in buildings, financial pressure exposes our spiritual weakness. Paul said, "I have learned the secret of being content" (Philippians 4:12). Key phrase: I have learned. Hardship enrolls us all in a basic contentment course, but we do not all get the same homework. Some of us learn through financial hardship and proving God's faithfulness for ourselves.' Donna Savage writes 'I've given God an "I can't do this" ultimatum more than once… I've also celebrated the adventure of moment-by-moment dependence on His resources. I've proved God's faithfulness in my prayers and in my pantry, and it's never limited by my bank balance.'

Day 46 - Matthew 6:30-33 (MSG)

Struggling? (Remember your everyday human concerns will be met!)

30-33 "If God gives such attention to the appearance of wildflowers—most of which are never even seen—don't you think he'll attend to you, take pride in you, do his best for you? What I'm trying to do here is to get you to relax, to not be so preoccupied with getting, so you can respond to God's giving. People who don't know God and the way he works fuss over these things, but you know both God and how he works. Steep your life in God-reality, God-initiative, God-provisions. Don't worry about missing out. You'll find all your every-day human concerns will be met.

Just an Observation

Pray, 'Heavenly Father, Your Word says, "Seek ye first the kingdom of God, and His righteousness; and all these things shall be added unto you." You are well able to take care of my financial situation; You know what needs to be done. Direct my steps (Proverbs 3:5-6). Help me to remember that Your resources are meant to flow freely from the place of abundance to the place of need (2 Corinthians 8:14). I believe You have a financial plan for my life, and when fear of the future threatens to overwhelm me, I will hope continually and praise You more and more (Psalms 71:14). As you walk with me through this crisis and I stay focused on You, you promised to keep me in perfect peace (Isaiah 26:3). Forgive me for worrying. I cast all my cares on you right now (1 Peter 5:7). I do not have to bear these burdens on my own…I lay them down and receive Your divine rest (Matthew 11:28). You promised to supply all my needs (Philippians 4:19); that it's Your good pleasure to give me the [blessings and benefits of Your] kingdom (Luke 12:32). You told me not to worry about anything and instead make my requests known to You with thanksgiving (Philippians 4:6-7). I know You'll take care of tomorrow because You're Jehovah-Jireh, my provider (Matthew 6:34). You know what I need and when I need it…You're the God of more than enough (Ephesians 3:20). Thank You for meeting my every need, and for the sense of peace and security You are imparting to me. In Jesus' name.

Day 47 – Isaiah 26:3-4 (GNT)

I might have fear BUT fear doesn't have me!

You, Lord, give perfect peace
   to those who keep their purpose firm
   and put their trust in you.
 Trust in the Lord forever;
   he will always protect us.

Just an Observation

I might have fear BUT fears don't have me. Fear is a normal part of living. And the most successful and confident people you know experience it. The difference is they refuse to be ruled by fear because they know that, when it gets out of control, it can paralyze you. The Bible says, '…fear hath torment…' (1 John 4:18). Neuroscientists at Yale University discovered that patients who expected to experience an electric shock had anxiety levels like those who responded to the real thing. Researcher Elizabeth Phelps writes, 'A lot of our fears and anxieties are learned through communication. If someone tells you to be afraid of a dog, then the brain responds as if you actually were.' In other words, our brains don't know the difference between real and imagined threats. This goes a long way toward explaining why the National Institute of Mental Health reported that almost twenty million Americans suffer from anxiety disorders. Someone who is perfectly safe, but has a fear of being robbed, suffers just as much as someone living in a situation with a high risk of robbery, or someone in the act of being robbed. Because our brains do not discriminate between emotions that are real or imagined, fear can dominate our lives, and it's just as devastating as physical injury. Psychologist Marilyn Barrick said, 'For the most part, fear is nothing but an illusion. When you share it with someone, it tends to disappear.' So, share your fears with God and watch them begin to disappear. The Bible says, 'You will keep in perfect peace all who trust in You, all whose thoughts are fixed on You!'

Day 48 – Mark 6:11 (GNT)

Shake it off

11 If you come to a town where people do not welcome you or will not listen to you, leave it and **shake the dust off** your feet. That will be a warning to them!

Just an Observation

Here is some good advice Jesus gave His disciples. When someone rejects you or will not listen to you, '…shake the dust off your feet when you leave, as a testimony against them.' When you experience rejection, you have two choices: allow it to affect your confidence and self-worth, or 'shake it off' and move on. Now, Jesus was not talking about sincere minds that do not understand, but proud minds that reject the truth. He was saying, 'Don't let it break your stride and keep you from accomplishing what needs to be done.' When Paul was shipwrecked on the island of Malta, he was bitten by a snake while gathering firewood. Immediately the islanders said to one another, '…this man is a murderer, whom, though he has escaped the sea, yet justice does not allow to live' (Acts 28:4 NKJV). How did Paul respond? '…he shook off the creature into the fire and suffered no harm' (v. 5 NKJV). What did the islanders say about him then? '…they changed their minds and said that he was a god' (v. 6 NKJV). Wow! People's minds change like the wind! So, do not let their compliments puff you up, or their criticisms tear you down. God's will is for you to help others. If they accept your help, give it. If not, go where you will be accepted and appreciated. Jesus said, '…I say to you, he who receives whomever I send, receives Me…' (John 13:20 NKJV). In the final analysis it is not you they are rejecting, but the One who sent you. Knowing that, gives you confidence and peace of mind.

Day 49 – Acts 17:28 (GNT)

Only God can fill the void

28 as someone has said,

'In him we live and move and exist.'

It is as some of your poets have said,

'We too are his children.'

Just an Observation

Ernest Gordon writes about American soldiers who were captured, tortured, and starved by the Japanese in the Malay Peninsula in World War II. As a result, they started acting like animals, clawing, fighting, and stealing food. To turn things around, the group decided to start reading the New Testament. And as Gordon read it to them, they were converted to Christ, and this community of animals was transformed into a community of love. That is because God lives in Jesus, and Jesus is willing to live in the hearts of those who trust Him. He offers joy, peace, a transformed life, and assurance of eternal life to all those who place their trust in His atoning death. So, what are you using to try to fill the void in your life? Material possessions, career success, and the pursuit of intellectual growth! You may as well give it up now—it will not work! Paul explained it like this to the philosophers in Athens: '…God…made the world and everything in it…He…gives life…to everything…He satisfies every need…His purpose was [that we should] seek after God…feel [our] way towards Him and find Him—though He is not far from…us. For in Him we live and move and exist…' (vv 24-28 NLT). In the words of the time-honored hymn: 'Now none but Christ can satisfy; none other name for me. There's love, and life, and lasting joy, Lord Jesus, found in Thee.'

Day 50 – Proverbs 2:6-8 (GNT)

Rules for Living

6 It is the Lord who gives wisdom; from him come knowledge and understanding. 7 He provides help and protection for those who are righteous and honest. 8 He protects those who treat others fairly, and guards those who are devoted to him.

Just an Observation

To succeed in life, try these things: **Decide what is important.** The story's told of a family who moved to the country to get away from the city. They decided to raise cattle, so they bought a ranch. One day a friend visited them and asked what they'd named it. Dad said, 'I wanted to call it The Flying-W, but Mom wanted to call it The Suzy-Q. One of our sons liked The Bar-J, but our daughter preferred The Lazy-Y. So, we compromised and called it The Flying-W, Suzy-Q, Bar-J, Lazy-Y Ranch.' The friend asked, 'How are your cattle doing?' Dad replied, 'We don't have any. They didn't survive the branding.' Come on; decide what is important to you! **Prioritize your time.** Too many of us are like the store owner who got so busy trying to keep the place clean that he forgot to open the front door. The reason you are in business is to serve customers and make a profit, not get distracted by secondary things. Base your life's decisions on your priorities. And if you need help figuring out what they are, ask God: 'For the Lord gives wisdom; from His mouth come knowledge and understanding.' **Learn to motivate yourself.** When tragedy struck his life, we read: 'David encouraged himself in the Lord...' (1 Samuel 30:6). You need to learn how to do that too. Jude writes: '...building up yourselves...praying in the Holy Ghost' (Jude v. 20). To succeed in life, you must learn to encourage yourself, pray and build yourself up.

Day 51 – Genesis 50:20 (GNT)

What about your dreams?

20 You plotted evil against me, but God turned it into good, in order to preserve the lives of many people who are alive today because of what happened.

Just an Observation

In the movie, "Up in the Air", actor George Clooney is hired by a major corporation to handle big layoffs. His job was to fire people. In one scene when he is about to fire an aging manager, he notices on the man's CV that he had been trained as a French chef. As the man expresses despair over losing his job, Clooney reminds him of his original dream and asks him this soul-searching question: 'Back when you started how much did it take to buy you away from your dream?' At that pivotal moment, the manager thought back to the time he decided to settle for a steady pay packet in exchange for what he really wanted to do with his life. Are you doing that? Understand this: the day you were born God had a track for you to run on and an assignment for you to fulfill. So, the question you must ask yourself is this: 'Is the difficult situation I'm in right now a God-given opportunity for me to go back and fulfill the dream God gave me in the first place?' Looking back on the most painful chapter in his life, when he was betrayed by his family, Joseph said, 'You intended to harm me, but God intended it for good.' His greatest loss led Joseph to the fulfillment of the dream God gave him in the beginning. Is that your story too? Are you realizing that you have settled for second best, and now God is giving you a second chance; a chance to do the thing He put you in the world to do? "I alone know the plans I have for you, plans to bring you prosperity and not disaster, plans to bring about the future you hope for." Jeremiah 29:11 GNT!

Day 52 – Matthew 18:15 (GNT)

Character, Courage and Caution

15 If your brother sins against you go to him and show him his fault. But do it privately, just between yourselves. If he listens to you, you have won your brother back.

Just an Observation

Jesus said, '…if your brother sins against you, go and tell him his fault between you and him alone. If he hears you, you have gained your brother.' Confronting someone requires three things: character, courage, and caution. (1) Character. Since Jesus was secure in His identity and character as God's Son, He was able to let go of the need to please and be accepted by those around Him. Being grounded in who you are in Christ and in what your heavenly Father created you to be, allows you the freedom to confront people when necessary without worrying about the fall-out or the negative consequences. (2) Courage. The Pharisees had the power to undermine Christ's reputation, which eventually led to His death on the cross. But He told them the truth, nonetheless. And you must do the same. You must be willing to take up your cross and follow Him, even when it means risking an argument and handling hurt feelings. To 'confront' means to get in 'front' of someone, look into their eyes, and deal with the issue honestly and lovingly because you value the relationship. (3) Caution. Make sure you are following God's timing and not your own. It is easy to use false courage or bravado to challenge others to get your own way. It is easy to claim a confrontation is necessary when what you want is control. No, you must ask God to show you when, how and where to confront others. Your goal should always be to reconcile and restore the relationship.

Day 53 – Proverbs 27:5-6 (GNT)

Correction

5 Better to correct someone openly than to let him think you don't care for him at all.

6 Friends mean well, even when they hurt you. But when an enemy puts his arm around your shoulder—watch out!

Just an Observation

The word 'correction' is not one we are always comfortable with. It sometimes recalls memories of frowning parents and painful consequences. Or we think of the risk of destroying a relationship rather than the possibilities of strengthening and enriching it. 'Faithful are the wounds of a friend, but the kisses of an enemy are deceitful.' We all need someone to tell us the truth because others have 20/20 vision where we have blind spots. Yes, someone may react defensively, but they may also be thrilled to realize you care more about their ultimate well-being than their immediate response to you. Corrections made from a loving spirit, not a self-righteous, 'I-know-what's-best' attitude are usually well received. If others sense you are genuinely concerned for them and long for a better relationship, they are likely to consider what you have to say and be open to making changes. Think of the courage Nathan the prophet showed in confronting David over his sin with Bathsheba. As king, David held the power of life and death over him. But Nathan loved David too much to allow sin to rob him of his destiny. God often uses us in each other's lives to restore us to the narrow yet rich paths of destiny that He has preordained. Looking back, David could say, 'Before I was afflicted, I went astray: but now have I kept thy word' (Psalms 119:67 AKJV). There are times when wisdom says, 'Mind your own business and stay out of it.' And there are other times when wisdom says, 'Because you love them, get involved.'

Day 54 – Luke 6:45 (GNT)

Self-Talk

45 A good person brings good out of the treasure of good things in his heart; a bad person brings bad out of his treasure of bad things. For the mouth speaks what the heart is full of.

Just an Observation

When John Roebling devised a plan to build a bridge between Manhattan and Brooklyn, experts thought it was impossible. They said a bridge spanning that distance could not withstand the winds and tides. But Roebling refused to concede defeat; instead, he and his son, Washington, worked to solve the problems. Then just as construction was about to start, Roebling was killed in an underwater accident that left his son brain-damaged and unable to walk or talk. The prevailing wisdom was to abandon the project, but Washington Roebling was determined to fulfill his father's dream. He developed a system of communication by touching a finger to his wife's arm, and she in turn conveyed his ideas to the project engineers. For thirteen years that is how he supervised construction—and in 1883 the first car drove across the Brooklyn Bridge. The 'impossible' had become reality! Are you facing a seemingly impossible situation at home, on the job, with your finances, or in a relationship? If so, what you tell yourself about it is important. Your self-talk sets you up for joy or misery. You can tell where your faith is by what comes out of your mouth: 'Good people bring good things out of the good they stored in their hearts…' (v 45 NCV). One pastor says: 'When the pressure's on, what comes out of your mouth lets you know if you need to make some adjustments…When you want something to show up in your outward man, deposit God's Word in the inward man. Feed on it continually…once you believe it, you'll find yourself saying it, and once you start saying it, your entire being will reflect the treasure of His Word inside.'

Day 55 – Luke 19:26 (GNT)

Out on a limb

26 'I tell you,' he replied, 'that to those who have something, even more will be given; but those who have nothing, even the little that they have will be taken away from them.

Just an Observation

As an Iowa farm boy, Robert Schuller remembers how his dad needed every particle of grain from the previous year's crop to feed his livestock. Nevertheless, there was always a little corner of the corn bin he refused to touch. When Schuller said, 'Dad, you still have grain in there,' his father would reply, 'That's next year's seed.' And when spring came, he planted it. Schuller writes: 'Suppose he'd studied the odds and said, "Let us see, I have a kernel of corn. I can feed it to the cattle, and I know it will be productive; there is no risk. Or I can bury it in the ground, but that is infinitely riskier. Weeds could choke it, birds could eat it, it might rot, or hail and winds could destroy it…on the other hand, it just might multiply a hundredfold." The Bible says, 'If you wait for perfect conditions, you'll never get anything done' (Ecclesiastes 11:4 TLB). Helen Keller said, 'Security is mostly a superstition. It doesn't exist in nature nor do the children of men as a whole experience it… Life is either a daring adventure, or nothing.' If you want 'more than you ever dreamed', you have got to go out on a limb. That is where the best fruit is. Acting in faith with no 'earthly' guarantee what is on the other side means attempting something you couldn't possibly do unless God gave you the ability. Jon Walker says: 'Faith grows when we take risks not just any kind of risks, but ones specifically directed by God. These God-nudges push us beyond the borders of our "independent states" into "the promised land" of life by faith.'

Day 56 – Philippians 2:14 (GNT)

Stop It!

14 Do everything without complaining or arguing.

Just an Observation

A lady who worked at the post office was approached by a customer who said, 'I can't write. Would you mind addressing this postcard for me?' After addressing it for him and writing a short message, the postal clerk asked, 'Is there anything else I can do for you, sir?' The man thought for a moment and said, 'Yes, could you add a P.S. at the end saying, "Please excuse the sloppy handwriting." Now, there's gratitude for you! The Bible says, 'Do all things without complaining' because when you do not, you end up hurting: (1) Yourself. Complaining leads to anger and depression. God loves you and He does not want you hurting yourself. (2) God. Complaining calls into question God's care, His character, and His competence. What you are saying is, 'Lord, you blew it! You had a chance to fulfil my demands and You chose not to.' (3) Others. Your words affect the people around you, and nobody enjoys spending time with a member of 'the cold-water bucket brigade'. Complaining temporarily satisfies our selfish nature, but it changes nothing. When you complain, you explain your pain for no gain. But here is the good news: The Bible says, '…the people became like those who complain of adversity' (Numbers 11:1 NAS). You did not start out as a complainer; you 'became' that way, and by God's grace you can become a thanksgiver! Once you acknowledge your habit of moaning and fault-finding, it becomes possible to choose a better one. A bad habit is like a nice soft bed; it's easy to get into and hard to get out of. So, if you have fallen into the habit of 'complaining'—stop it!

Day 57 – Numbers 11:1 (GNT)

Stop complaining!

The people began to complain to the Lord about their troubles. When the Lord heard them, he became angry and sent fire on the people. It burned among them and destroyed one end of the camp.

Just an Observation

If you think complaining is no big deal, read this: '…when the people complained…the Lord heard…and His anger was aroused. So, the fire of the Lord burned among them, and consumed some in the outskirts of the camp.' A wise man once said, 'I complained that I had no shoes, until I met a man who had no feet.' God has blessed us in 101 different ways, and He does not want to hear us whining. What were the Israelites grumbling about anyway? 'Adversity' (NAS). For some of us adversity comes through illness. For others it's a faltering career, not enough money to pay the bills, or a family situation that happened years ago and now you're left shouldering the responsibility. Some of us made poor decisions earlier in life, and as a result our plans fell apart. Now we are struggling with marital problems, blended families, and the consequences of our choices. We all must deal with some level of adversity. We each have something in our life that God does not want to hear us griping about! Understand this: it is hard to live with adversity, but when you complain, you forego the grace that'll get you through it. By choosing to complain and cling to the image of a perfect life, you forfeit the grace that is available to you and will bring you victory. So, change your way of thinking. Get down on your knees and pray: 'Lord, I want the landscape of my life to be different; to experience the joy You give to those who leave the wilderness of ingratitude and move into the Promised Land of thanksgiving.' That is a prayer that will change you!

Day 58 – 2 Kings 5:11-13 (GNT)

Inflexible?

¹¹ But Naaman left in a rage, saying, "I thought that he would at least come out to me, pray to the LORD his God, wave his hand over the diseased spot, and cure me! ¹² Besides, aren't the rivers Abana and Pharpar, back in Damascus, better than any river in Israel? I could have washed in them and been cured!"

¹³ His servants went up to him and said, "Sir, if the prophet had told you to do something difficult, you would have done it. Now why can't you just wash yourself, as he said, and be cured?"

Just an Observation

As a general in the Syrian army, Naaman was accustomed to having things his own way. So, when Elisha told him to dip seven times in the muddy Jordan River to be healed of leprosy, he 'went away in a rage'. He said, 'Aren't there cleaner rivers? Couldn't the prophet just lay hands on me and heal me?' Fortunately, he listened to his servants, swallowed his pride and received a miracle. There are important lessons here. Since all progress calls for adapting to change and overcoming obstacles, ask yourself - (1) What is at the core of my fear and anger over this situation? Am I afraid of the unknown and the changes it may bring? (2) Am I being inflexible and trying to impose my will and wishes in this situation? Am I willing to forfeit God's perfect will by resisting a change He is orchestrating? Many of us miss God's best. Why? Like Naaman, we are accustomed to being waited on and having our ego stroked. E.G.O. means Edging God Out! Are you doing that? (3) Am I being lazy or incompetent, not wanting to invest the necessary time and effort into the change? Unless you are willing to change, you will not grow. And if you do not grow, you will not position yourself to receive the blessing God has in mind for you. Charles Franklin Kettering said, 'The world hates change, yet it is the only thing that has brought progress.' Today ask God for the emotional and spiritual strength to embrace the changes He is bringing into your life, and to help you see them as being for your good (Romans 8:28).

Day 59 – Psalm 34:9 (GNT)

The flint, the sponge and the honeycomb!

Honor the Lord, all his people;
  those who obey him have all they need.

Just an Observation

There are three kinds of givers: the flint, the sponge, and the honeycomb. To get even a spark from a flint you must hammer it. To get anything out of a sponge you must squeeze it. But a honeycomb just overflows with sweetness. So which kind of giver are you? The Psalmist writes, 'Taste and see that the Lord is good; blessed is the man who takes refuge in Him…for those who fear Him lack nothing' (vv 8-9 NIV). Tithing is an act of worship. Of the 118 hours you are awake each week, almost half are involved in earning money. So, when you give God your money, you are giving Him your brain, your brawn and yourself. When you go to the Lord's house on the Lord's Day, partake of the Lord's Supper and put the Lord's tithe into the Lord's treasury, it is an act of profound worship. Now, let us be clear: A God who paves heaven's streets with gold is not going to go broke because you don't give Him a tithe of your income. But you might! This sign appeared on a church marquee: 'Give God a tithe in proportion to thine income, lest He be displeased with thee and give thee an income in proportion to thy tithe.' The act of tithing is not about the tithe; it is about the tither. It is not about the gift; it is about the giver. It is not about the money; it is about the man or woman. It is not about possessions; it is about the possessor. As the songwriter Isaac Watts said, 'Were the whole realm of nature mine; that were an offering far too small. Love so amazing, so divine, demands my soul, my life, my all.'

Day 60 - Galatians 6:2 (GNT)

Surround yourself with people who believe in you!

Help carry one another's burdens, and in this way, you will obey the law of Christ.

Just an Observation

Mark Twain said, 'Keep away from people who try to belittle your ambitions. Small people always do that, but the really great make you feel that you, too, can become great.' Why does the Bible say, 'Carry each other's burdens'? Because one person can only carry a burden so far on their own! American novelist John Kennedy Toole quickly discovered that. As a young writer he worked alone writing a novel in New Orleans. When it was finished, he sent it to publisher after publisher, but they all turned him down. Overcome by rejection, he took his own life. Sometime after the funeral, his mother found a coffee-stained manuscript in the attic and took it to a professor at Louisiana State University who agreed to read it. Immediately he recognized its genius and recommended it to a major publisher. After its release, John Kennedy Toole's novel, A Confederacy of Dunces, won a Pulitzer Prize and was heralded as one of the major novels of the twentieth century. If only he had surrounded himself with friends who knew how to share his burden, encourage him when he faced rejection and motivate him to keep going, his life would have turned out very differently. So, the word for you today is—'Surround yourself with people who believe in you.' Encourage and support them and welcome their support in return. Spend more time with those who sharpen you and make you better, and less time with those who drain your energy, time, and talent. The truth is friends who speak encouragement into your life are priceless. Their words are 'Like apples of gold in settings of silver…' (Proverbs 25:11 NIV).

Day 61 - Philippians 4:7-8 (GNT)

Keeping a Good Attitude

7 And God's peace, which is far beyond human understanding, will keep your hearts and minds safe in union with Christ Jesus.

8 In conclusion, my friends, fill your minds with those things that are good and that deserve praise: things that are true, noble, right, pure, lovely, and honorable. 9 Put into practice what you learned and received from me, both from my words and from my actions. And the God who gives us peace will be with you.

Just an Observation

When you're going through bad times, your goal should be to keep a good attitude. And with God's help you can. Dr Viktor Frankl, a Nazi Holocaust camp survivor, said: 'If a prisoner felt that he could no longer endure the realities of camp life, he found a way out in his mental life—an invaluable opportunity to dwell in the spiritual domain, the one that the SS was unable to destroy. Spiritual life strengthened the prisoner, helped him to adapt, and thereby improved his chances of survival.' Some practical advice on keeping a good attitude in bad times: (1) believe the best about others but do not get bent out of shape when they disappoint you. Nobody is perfect, including you. Just be grateful for the people that bring joy and endeavor to be counted among them. (2) When you are tempted to retaliate, judge, or become impatient, say to yourself, 'This is an opportunity for me to model a great attitude for the Glory of God.' You say, 'But this person is driving me crazy.' Then refuse to be a 'passenger' and go along with them. Take back the wheel, get into the driver's seat of your life, and determine which direction you will go and what attitude you will have. The Bible says: '…whatever things are true, whatever things are noble, whatever things are just, whatever things are pure, whatever things are lovely, whatever things are of good report, if there is any virtue and if there is anything praiseworthy—meditate on these things…and the God of peace will be with you.'

Day 62 – 1 John 4:18 (GNT)

Forgiveness, Grace and Mercy

18 There is no fear in love; perfect love drives out all fear. So then, love has not been made perfect in anyone who is afraid, because fear has to do with punishment.

Just an Observation

God cares about you too much to leave you in any doubt about His love. The Bible says His 'perfect love expels all fear'. If God loved us with an imperfect love, we would have cause to worry. Human love is flawed; it keeps a checklist of our sins and shortcomings—and consults it often. God keeps no such list. His love casts out our fear because it casts out our guilt. John writes, '…if our heart condemns us, God is greater than our heart…' (1 John 3:20 NKJV). When you feel unforgiven, question your feelings but do not question God. Go back to His Word; it outranks self-criticism and self-doubt. Nothing fosters confidence like a clear grasp of God's grace, and nothing fosters fear like ignorance of it. The fact is if you have not accepted God's grace, you are doomed to live in fear. No pill, pep talk, psychiatrist or earthly possession can put your mind at ease. Those things may help numb your fear, but they cannot eradicate it. Only God's grace can do that. Have you accepted Christ's forgiveness? If not, get down on your knees and do it now. The Bible says, 'If we confess our sins, He is faithful and just to forgive us…and to cleanse us from all unrighteousness' (1 John 1:9). The place of confession is also the place of cleansing and restored confidence towards God. Your prayer can be as simple as this: 'Lord, I admit I've turned away from You. Please forgive me. I place my soul in Your hands and my trust in Your grace. In Jesus' name I pray. Amen.' Now, having received God's forgiveness, mercy, and grace—live like it!

Day 63 – Psalm 3:2-4 (GNT)

God won't give up on you!

They talk about me and say,
  "God will not help him."
3 But you, O Lord, are always my shield from danger;
  you give me victory
  and restore my courage.
4 I call to the Lord for help,
  and from his sacred hill he answers me.

Just an Observation

Regardless of how badly we have failed or how often we have failed God won't give up on us. So, do not give up on yourself! Nothing you have done is beyond the scope of His grace. Others may give up on you, but not God. King David fell as low as a person can get. He was guilty of adultery, deception and murder, all major offenses. But God forgave and restored him. He writes about it in two Psalms. In the first Psalm he writes: 'Many are saying of me, God will not deliver him. But You, Lord, are a shield around me, O Lord; You bestow glory on me and lift my head. To the Lord I cry aloud, and He answers me from His holy hill. I lie down and sleep; I wake again because the Lord sustains me. I will not fear the tens of thousands drawn up against me on every side…From the Lord comes deliverance' (vv 2-7 NIV). In the next Psalm he writes: '…He turned to me and heard my cry. He lifted me out of the slimy pit, out of the mud and mire; He set my feet on a rock and gave me a firm place to stand. He put a new song in my mouth, a hymn of praise to our God. Many will see and fear the Lord and put their trust in Him' (Psalm 40:1-3 NIV). And the God who turned David's greatest mess into a message, and his greatest test into a testimony, will do the same for you when you turn to Him and receive His forgiveness, mercy, and grace.

Day 64 – Proverbs 15:31-32 (GNT)

OWN IT

31 If you pay attention when you are corrected, you are wise.

32 If you refuse to learn, you are hurting yourself. If you accept correction, you will become wiser.

Just an Observation

Despite his faults, flaws and failures, God called David '…a man after [my] own heart…' (Acts 13:22). And one of the qualities that made David great was his willingness to acknowledge his mistakes. Here were two instances of it: 1) When fleeing the wrath of King Saul, he sought the help of a certain priest—a decision that caused Saul to order the death of eighty-five priests and their families. Devastated but not defensive, David told the surviving son of the slain priest who had assisted him, '…I have caused the death of all your father's family' (1 Samuel 22:22 NLT). Can you imagine taking responsibility for such a tragic consequence? 2) When the prophet Nathan confronted him about his affair with Bathsheba and his attempt to cover up her resulting pregnancy by having her husband killed, David acknowledged, '…I have sinned against the Lord…' (2 Samuel 12:13 NLT). Would you have the emotional and spiritual maturity to make such an admission? Or do you tend to defend your actions for fear of being judged, criticized, or rejected? Do you sometimes feel attacked when someone offers feedback, whether it is positive or negative? Do you retreat in silence? Do you counter-accuse or blame your attacker? Do you make hostile comments? Do you become sarcastic? Making mistakes does not make you a lesser person but defending them do. Do not let pride rob you of the wisdom that comes from acknowledging your mistakes and ultimately growing through them. 'He who disdains instruction despises his own soul, but he who heeds rebuke gets understanding.'

Day 65 – Jeremiah 18:1-6 (GNT)

Clay in the Potter's Hand

The Lord said to me, 2 "Go down to the potter's house, where I will give you my message." 3 So I went there and saw the potter working at his wheel. 4 **Whenever a piece of pottery turned out imperfect, he would take the clay and make it into something else.** 5 Then the Lord said to me, 6 "Don't I have the right to do with you people of Israel what the potter did with the clay? You are in my hands just like clay in the potter's hands.

Just an Observation

Henry Poppen, one of China's first missionaries, spent forty years telling its people about the love of Jesus and how He died to take away their sin. One day, after he had finished speaking, a man approached him and said, 'We know this Jesus! He's been here.' Dr Poppen explained how that was not possible because Jesus had lived and died long ago in a country far from China. 'Oh no,' the man insisted, 'He died here. I can even show you his grave.' He led Dr. Poppen outside the city to a cemetery where an American was buried. There, inscribed on a crumbling gravestone was the name of a medical doctor who felt called by God to live and die among the people of this remote Chinese village. And when its people heard Dr Poppen describe the attributes of Jesus—His mercy, His love, His kindness, His willingness to forgive—they remembered the missionary doctor. God will use you when you are willing to become 'clay in the potter's hand'. Clay has no aspirations; it is moldable, pliable, and completely subject to the potter's will. Henry Blackaby says: 'When God's assignment demands humility, He finds a servant willing to be humbled. When it requires zeal, He looks for someone He can fill with His Spirit. God uses holy vessels, so He finds those who will allow Him to remove their impurities. It is not a noble task being clay. There's no glamour to it, nothing boast-worthy, except it's exactly what God's looking for.'

Day 66 – 1 Corinthians 13:7 (GNT)

Beware of cynicism

7 Love never gives up; and its faith, hope, and patience never fail.

Just an Observation

There are very few monuments erected to sceptics. That is because instead of building people up, they tear them down. David's older brother Eliab was like that. Here is his story. When nobody else in Saul's army, including Eliab, who was a general, was willing to take on Goliath, David volunteered to go out and fight this 'uncircumcised Philistine' (1 Samuel 17:36). In Bible times circumcision was a sign of God's covenant of protection and provision for the Israelites. And David knew this bully had no such contract with God; only the Israelites could claim such a benefit. As a result, David was very secure in the covenant, and embraced God's promise. Obviously, this was not the case for Eliab. His 'anger burned against David and he said: "Why have you come down? And with whom have you left those few sheep in the wilderness? I know your insolence and the wickedness of your heart; for you have come down in order to see the battle"' (v. 28 NASB). Interestingly, the name Eliab means 'God is my Father', so Eliab not only represents secular cynics, but Christian ones too. Yes, we have them in the Church! All it takes is one skeptical member and soon all those with weaker faith, or no faith at all, start chiming in and perpetuating the negativity. Beware: cynicism can wreak havoc in any relationship and environment. That is why the Bible says, 'Blessed is the man who doesn't sit in the seat of the scornful' (Psalm 1:1). Think twice before sitting down in that seat. If you stay, there too long you may not be able to get up again!

Day 67 – Matthew 6:33 (GNT)

Quiet Time

33 Instead, be concerned above everything else with the Kingdom of God and with what he requires of you, and he will provide you with all these other things.

Just an Observation

Jesus said, 'Seek first the kingdom of God and His righteousness, and all these things shall be added to you.' What kind of 'things' was He talking about? Things like money, houses, relationships, health, and jobs. What did He mean by 'the kingdom of God'? Living under the rule of Christ each moment and submitting to His will in all things. When Jesus used the word 'seek', He called for three things: (1) Intentional. When something important is lost, you must put aside other things and seek until you find it. (2) Importance. Position, performance, prosperity, and popularity can be good things when safely used. But without the rule of Christ in your life, you will always be vulnerable to the devil. (3) Importunity. No matter how long it takes, how hard you must work or what you must rearrange; restore your quiet time with God to its rightful place. The psalmist wrote, 'When You said, "Seek My face," My heart said to You, "Your face, LORD, I will seek"' (Psalm 27:8 NKJV). 'Quiet time' has been called many things throughout the history of the Church: morning watch, daily devotions, appointment with God, or personal devotional time. It really does not matter what you call it, if you have it regularly. Your quiet time with God is just daily fellowship with Him through His Word and prayer. It is a time you deliberately set aside to meet with Him. The goal is that you might grow in your personal relationship with God so that you can know Him, love Him, serve Him, and become more like Him.

Day 68 – Luke 6:12 (GNT)

Quiet Time with God

12 At that time Jesus went up a hill to pray and spent the whole night there praying to God.

Just an Observation

Why do you need a quiet time with God each day? Because Jesus did, and He is our example: 'He was up long before daybreak and went…to pray' (Mark 1:35 TLB). The truth is, we make time for what we value most, for the people we love most, for our highest priorities, and what we find most rewarding. Notice, Jesus seldom prayed for anybody in public. Why? Because He'd already done His praying before He got there! He made deposits each morning so that He could make withdrawals all day long. And the busier He got, the more He prayed. Did He know something we do not? Jesus had no difficulty choosing between the crowd's agenda and His Father's will. 'I can do nothing on my own. I judge as God tells me. Therefore, my judgment is just, because I carry out the will of the one who sent me' (John 5:30 NLT). Why do spiritual leaders sometimes fall? Because they get caught up in the work of the Lord and neglect their relationship with Him. Throughout history, anyone who has been greatly used by God was a person of prayer. Martin Luther said, 'I have so much to do that I must spend the first three hours each day in prayer.' Ceaseless activity will drain you and leave you vulnerable to Satan's attack. The sign on a church bulletin board says it all: 'Seven prayerless days make one weak Christian.' So, the busier you become, the more time you need to spend with God. Simply stated: if you are too busy to have a quiet time with God, you are too busy!

Day 69 – Job 23:12 (GNT)

Making time for God

I always do what God commands;
  I follow his will, not my own desires.

Just an Observation

Your quiet time with God is more than just a good idea, it is vital to your spiritual survival. It is also essential to your spiritual growth and maturity. You say, 'But I go to church every week.' Can you imagine what would happen if you ate only once a week? The patriarch Job said, 'I have…treasured his words more than daily food.' Peter described the Scriptures as nourishing milk (1 Peter 2:2), and the writer to the Hebrews called the Word of God solid food (Hebrews 5:14). Your quiet time is also like a spiritual bath. Jesus said, 'Now ye are clean through the word which I have spoken unto you' (John 15:3 KJV). You shower every day to stay clean and avoid body odor. It is not easy to be around someone who smells badly, and you run the risk of offending them by telling them so. But if you love them, you will do it. Jesus told Peter, 'Thou art an offence unto me: for thou savourest not the things that be of God, but those that be of men' (Matthew 16:23 KJV). Here is the bottom line. Unless you protect your quiet time with God: you will be cut off from your source of strength, guidance, and wisdom; your usefulness to God will be limited and you'll be inconsistent in your Christian life. You say, 'But I don't have time!' You have the same 168 hours each week that everybody else has! And how you spend them is determined by what you think is most important. So, if you think being in fellowship with God is important, begin to make time for it.

Day 70 – Matthew 5:5 (GNT)

Gentleness

Happy are those who are humble;

they will receive what God has promised!

Just an Observation

Jesus said, 'Blessed are the gentle, for they shall inherit the earth'. We'd all be a lot better off if gentle people ran the world, because those who aren't gentle are making a real mess of things! St Francis de Sales said, 'Nothing is as strong as gentleness, and nothing as gentle as real strength.' Just as you catch more flies with honey than with vinegar, people respond more readily to gentleness than aggressiveness. The famous football coach, John Wooden, told the following story: 'My dad, Joshua Wooden, was a strong man in one sense, but a gentle man. He could lift heavy things men half his age couldn't, but he would also read poetry to us each night after a day working in the fields raising corn, hay, wheat, tomatoes, and watermelons. We had a team of mules named Jack and Kate on our farm. Kate would often get stubborn and lie down on me when I was plowing. I couldn't get her up no matter how roughly I treated her. Dad would see my predicament and walk across the field until he got close enough to say, "Kate." Then she would get up and start working again. He never touched her in anger. It took me a long time to understand that even a stubborn mule responds to gentleness.' When the Bible speaks of meekness, it's not speaking of weakness. Meekness means 'power under control'. An unbroken horse is useless; an overdose of medicine kills rather than cures; wind out of control destroys everything in its path. Jesus was powerful but He was gentle. And you are called to follow in His footsteps (1 Peter 2:21).

Day 71 – Hebrews 3:1 (GNT)

It's in your mind

My Christian friends, who also have been called by God! Think of Jesus, whom God sent to be the High Priest of the faith we profess.

Just an Observation

I've been trying to lose weight, but I love sweets. How can you overcome temptation? By repeating, 'I must not eat sweets, I must not eat sweets, I must not eat sweets'? No, the more you think about sweets, the more you're going to want them. Instead, you must focus on something else (or someone else – Jesus!) who can help you overcome the temptation. The problem is not in the sweets shop, it's in your mind. That's where victory is won or lost. Paul writes: 'Dear brothers and sisters, I plead with you to give your bodies to God because of all he has done for you. Let them be a living and holy sacrifice – the kind he will find acceptable. This is truly the way to worship him. Don't copy the behavior and customs of this world, but let God transform you into a new person by changing the way you think. Then you will learn to know God's will for you, which is good and pleasing and perfect' (Romans 12:1-2 NLT). You can lock yourself up in a room and still think about sweets. On the other hand, you can get your mind on Jesus, draw strength from Him, and drive victoriously past every sweet shop in town. The same principle applies to any habit you want to break and any sin you want to conquer. Does victory come easily, or overnight? No, Satan tempted Jesus repeatedly in the wilderness, and he'll keep tempting us until he realizes his strategies no longer work. 'Then the devil left Him, and behold, angels came and ministered to Him' (Matthew 4:11 NKJV). Through Christ, we can conquer our habits.

Day 72 – Genesis 50:20(GNT)

The right Response

20 You plotted evil against me, but God turned it into good, in order to preserve the lives of many people who are alive today because of what happened.

Just an Observation

Twenty-two years after selling Joseph into slavery, his brothers now stand before him as prime minister of Egypt. They don't recognize him, and he holds their fate in his hands. If you'd been in his shoes, what would you have done? Gotten even? Reminded them of their past offences? For the next few days, let's look at what Joseph did: He didn't talk about it. 'There was no one with Joseph when he made himself known to his brothers' (Genesis 45:1 NIV). Joseph made sure no one in Egypt would ever know what they'd done to him. And isn't that how God treats us? The fact is He has enough on each of us to bury us, yet He refuses to resurrect our past sins. So why do we? To punish! 'Perfect love drives out fear, because fear has to do with punishment' (1 John 4:18 NIV). What are we afraid of? That they'll get away with it. We want them punished, so we tell everybody what happened. And when we do: We play God! God says, 'Vengeance is mine; I will repay' (Romans 12:19 KJV). He alone knows the weakness in your offenders that caused them to hurt you, and whether they've repented and changed. We set the standard by which we ourselves will be judged. 'You will be judged in the same way that you judge others' (Matthew 7:2 NCV). If that's a truth you're not comfortable with: 'Get rid of all bitterness…Instead, be kind to each other, tenderhearted, and forgiving one another, just as God…has forgiven you' (Ephesians 4:31-32 NLT). When you've been wronged, 'forgive and forget' is the right response!

Day 73 – **Romans 8:15 (GNT)**

Restoration, not revenge

15 For the Spirit that God has given you does not make you slaves and cause you to be afraid; instead, the Spirit makes you God's children, and by the Spirit's power we cry out to God, "Father! my Father!"

Just an Observation

Joseph's brothers 'were…stunned with surprise. "Come over here," he said. So, they came closer. And he said again, "I am Joseph, your brother whom you sold into Egypt! But don't be angry with yourselves that you did this to me, for God did it!"' (Genesis 45:3-5 TLB). You'll notice that Joseph didn't react the way we so often do when someone hurts us. He didn't: 1) distance his brothers; 2) enjoy watching them squirm; 3) practice one-upmanship; 4) gloat and say 'gotcha!'; 5) remind them of how they'd put him down and despised his dreams; 6) demand they acknowledge that he was right, and they were wrong; 7) say, 'I told you so!' No, Joseph wanted to be loved, not feared. He wanted restoration, not revenge. He knew that the long-term benefits of healing a relationship far outweighed any short-term satisfaction you get from retaliation. He understood that it's only by releasing your offender that you set yourself free. The Bible says, 'You did not receive a spirit…to fear, but…the Spirit of sonship. And by him we cry, "Abba, Father."' The word 'Abba' is a term of endearment which means 'Daddy'. God doesn't bring up your past or keep you at arm's length because of your failures. He wants you to know you can come to Him at any time, know that you're accepted, feel secure in His presence, and call Him 'Daddy'. And that's the kind of love He wants you to show to others – a love that doesn't want them to feel afraid in your presence.

Day 74 – Genesis 45:5 (NLT)

Cut it loose

5 But don't be upset, and don't be angry with yourselves for selling me to this place. It was God who sent me here ahead of you to preserve your lives.

Just an Observation

Joseph told his brothers, 'Don't be angry with yourselves that you did this to me…God has sent me here to keep you and your families alive, so that you will become a great nation' (vv. 5, 7 TLB). When are we most likely to lay a guilt trip on others? When we've forgotten the grace, we ourselves received from God. Often, it's your forgiveness that makes it possible for others to forgive themselves! Self-forgiveness is a high hurdle for most of us. Paul wrote, 'I…wasted [the Church]' (Galatians 1:13 KJV). Now he goes back to those same towns and preaches, and who is in the audience? The widows and orphans! If Paul had not learned to receive God's grace, he could never have fulfilled God's will. Some ancient societies punished murderers by strapping the victim to their back. Paul may have had this in mind when he wrote, 'Who will deliver me from this body of death?' (Romans 7:24 NKJV). Nothing is heavier than guilt. Guilt will drag you down; cause you to leave a bad taste wherever you go. Even your friends will become exhausted and say, 'Get over it,' destroy your relationships. Who wants to be around someone who is obsessed with a corpse? You would only be using the new relationship to numb the pain of the old one and destroy your health, because you aren't built to carry resentment. Cut it loose! Somebody said, 'Everyone should have a special cemetery lot in which to bury the faults of friends and loved ones.' Grieve if you need to – then bury it and move on!

Day 75 – Titus 3:2 (GNT)

Say Thank You

2 Tell them not to speak evil of anyone, but to be peaceful and friendly, and always to show a gentle attitude toward everyone.

Just an Observation

Gratitude comes with a host of benefits. It improves your heart rhythm, reduces stress, and helps you heal physically and think more clearly under pressure. It floods your body and brain with endorphins that strengthen and rejuvenate you. And like any muscle, the more you exercise it the stronger it grows. It doesn't have to be complicated; just take a walk and think about your blessings and it will set the tone for your day. The psalmist said, 'Praise the Lord and do not forget all his kindnesses' (Psalm 103:2 NCV). God's blessings operate 24 hours a day, 365 days a year. Try this: When you sit down to eat, have everyone at the table name something they're thankful for. There's always something. My grandma use to say; 'I thank you, Lord, for my nine good teeth, four upper and five lower!' Psychologist Martin Seligman suggests sending a letter or email of gratitude to somebody, then visiting that person and reading it to them. People who say 'thank you' are measurably happier and less depressed. The CEO of Campbell Soup wrote over sixteen thousand thank-you notes to his employees and energized the entire company in the process. Go ahead, encourage your family, friends and co-workers by letting them know you appreciate what they do. The Bible says, 'God's people should be bighearted and courteous.' One author observes: 'You have it in your power to increase the sum of the world's happiness by giving a few words of sincere appreciation to someone who's lonely or discouraged. Perhaps you'll forget the kind words you say today, but the recipient may cherish them for a lifetime.'

Day 76 – Ephesians 5:1-2(MSG)

A New Level of Forgiveness

1-2 Watch what God does, and then you do it, like children who learn proper behavior from their parents. Mostly what God does is love you. Keep company with him and learn a life of love. Observe how Christ loved us. His love was not cautious but extravagant. He didn't love in order to get something from us but to give everything of himself to us. ***Love like that.***

Just an Observation

Imagine how Joseph's brothers felt when he said, 'It was not you who sent me here, but God' (Genesis 45:8 NKVJ). Is he serious? God did it? This is a new level of forgiveness! Preserving the dignity and self-worth of others that's what God does with us! With full knowledge of our sinful past, He covers us with the garment of grace. And He expects us to do the same for others. As you read the genealogy of Jesus in Matthew chapter one, you might think the sin of adultery between David and Bathsheba was part of the divine strategy all along. No, sin never is, and David paid a high price. Yet the Bible records these events as though they were supposed to have happened in just that way. The Bible says, 'Be full of love for others, following the example of Christ who loved you and gave himself to God as a sacrifice to take away your sins. And God was pleased.' When you truly forgive, there's no place for self-righteousness. You're able to forgive because you remember what you yourself have been forgiven of; you acknowledge what you're capable of; and you see God's hand at work in the bigger picture. Joseph wasn't being condescending or patronizing, nor was he thinking, 'I'll be admired for being so gracious.' No, during his years in prison God had moved on his heart and changed his attitude. So, when Joseph said, 'You meant evil against me; but God meant it for good' (Genesis 50:20 NKJV), he really meant it! That kind of response takes forgiveness to a whole new level!

Day 77 – Genesis 45:10-11 (GNT)

Did you forgive?

10 You can live in the region of Goshen, where you can be near me—you, your children, your grandchildren, your sheep, your goats, your cattle, and everything else that you have. 11 If you are in Goshen, I can take care of you. There will still be five years of famine; and I do not want you, your family, and your livestock to starve.'"

Just an Observation

Not only did Joseph forgive his brothers, but he also protected them from their worst nightmare having to go back and tell their ageing father what they'd done twenty-two years earlier. Joseph is a step ahead of them; he tells them what to say and what not to say: 'Go up to my father, and say to him, "Thus says your son Joseph: 'God has made me lord of all Egypt; come…You shall dwell in the land of Goshen, and you shall be near to me, you and your children…I will provide for you'"' (vv. 9-11 NKJV). You might say, 'I think they should have been forced to confess what they'd done.' No, that would have given their father Jacob an even greater burden to bear; he would have been struggling with regret over his lost years with Joseph and not to mention having to fight bitterness towards his other sons. Joseph was wise and it made his brothers respect him more. There's a big difference between confessing and 'dumping'. Irreparable damage can be done when you try to get relief by dumping the details of your guilt on somebody who can't handle them. After David sinned with Bathsheba he wrote, 'Against You [God], You only, have I sinned' (Psalm 51:4 NKJV). When you consider that God knows all about your sin yet promises to keep it a closely guarded secret, it should: increase your sense of humility and gratitude; cause you to keep your mouth shut; and make you refuse to hold anybody else sins and shortcomings over their head. If Joseph can forgive, you can too.

Day 78 – Genesis 20:21 (GNT)

Walk in Forgiveness

21 You have nothing to fear. I will take care of you and your children." So, he reassured them with kind words that touched their hearts.

Just an Observation

Seventeen years after being reunited with Joseph, his long-lost son, Jacob died, and Joseph's brothers panicked. They started to think, 'Now Joseph will pay us back for all the evil we did to him' (v. 15 TLB). So, they got together, made up a story, and sent word to Joseph, saying, 'Before your father died, he instructed us to say to you: "Please forgive your brothers for the great wrong they did to you"' (vv. 16-17 NLT). Now think about it. If their father really had said this, he wouldn't have told Joseph's brothers, he'd have told Joseph himself, right? He wouldn't have gone to his grave with the fear that Joseph might exact revenge. When Joseph heard that his brothers doubted his forgiveness he called them together and wept, saying, '"Don't be afraid…I myself will take care of you and your families." …And he spoke very kindly to them, reassuring them' (v. 21 TLB). True forgiveness, the kind that's taught in Scripture, is a commitment you must practice every day of your life. People need loving the most, when they deserve it the least. No one ever said it would be easy. If Jesus had waited until His enemies repented, He'd never have prayed on the cross: 'Father, forgive them, for they do not know what they do' (Luke 23:34 NKJV). Sure, it's easier to forgive when others acknowledge their offence. But if that's a prerequisite, you may never experience victory! And what you don't forgive – you must relive! So, for your own sake forgive, take back your life, and begin walking in the blessing of the Lord.

Day 79 – Genesis 2:5 (GNT)

Are you in place?

5 there were no plants on the earth and no seeds had sprouted, because he had not sent any rain, and there was no one to cultivate the land.

Just an Observation

The Bible says, 'The Lord God had not caused it to rain upon the earth, and there was not a man to till the ground.' At the beginning of creation God caused a mist to come up from the earth and water the ground. Up until that time there had been no downpour from the heavens. That's because there was nobody to do the prep work and 'till the ground'. There's a spiritual lesson here! There are things God has planned to do, made provision for, and desires to do but He won't until we 'get into place' where we can receive what He longs to give us. The blessing is there, safe in God's keeping. The need is there, persistent in its pain. But the blessing can't come until your heart is in the right place for God to act. Right now, you may be enjoying a 'mist', but you know God has more for you. You may have a frustration that causes you to say, 'Why am I not further along?' Rather than blaming people and circumstances, you need to pause, look up, and ask, 'Lord, are You waiting for me to get into place?' When you ask that question, be prepared to hear the answer and obey it, even if it means rearranging your priorities and paying the price to receive what God wants you to have. What does He want you to have? Not a mist, but a downpour! He's willing and 'able to do exceedingly abundantly above all that we ask or think, according to the power that worketh in us' (Ephesians 3:20 KJV). But first we must 'get into place'.

Day 80 – Ephesians 6:18 (GNT)

Prayer changes things and people

18 Do all this in prayer, asking for God's help. Pray on every occasion, as the Spirit leads. For this reason, keep alert and never give up; pray always for all God's people.

Just an Observation

In Scripture there are many kinds of prayer. Let's look at some of them and see what we can learn: 1) **The prayer of surrender.** When Paul met Christ on the Damascus Road he prayed, 'Lord, what wilt thou have me to do?' (Acts 9:6 KJV). That's like signing your name to a blank check and saying, 'Here I am, Lord, do with me as You please. I hope I like what You choose, but even if I don't, I'll do it anyway; Your will be done, not mine.' You're deciding to voluntarily follow God rather than trying to get Him to follow you. As a result, He will do the work that needs to be done in you, so that He can do the work He desires to do through you. 2) **The prayer of commitment.** The Bible says, 'Casting the whole of your care [all your anxieties, all your worries, all your concerns, once and for all] on Him' (1 Peter 5:7 AMP). If you keep trying to control everything, your stress levels will keep mounting. But once you learn to hand things over to God, you'll wonder why you spent even a single day worrying. 3) **The prayer of intercession.** The prophet Ezekiel writes, 'I looked for someone…who would…stand before me in the gap on behalf of the land' (Ezekiel 22:30 NIV). 'The gap' is the distance between what is and what can be. And when there's a 'gap' in someone's relationship with God due to a sin, as a believer you have the privilege (and responsibility) of placing yourself in that gap and praying for them. 4) **The prayer of petition**. You must learn to be confident in asking God to meet your needs. Jesus promised, 'What things so ever ye desire, when ye pray, believe that ye receive them, and ye shall have them' (Mark 11:24 KJV). If we'd stop trying to impress God, we'd be a lot better off. Length, loudness, or eloquence isn't the issue; it's the sincerity of our heart, the faith that's in our heart, and the assurance that we're praying according to God's will that gets results. 5) **The prayer of agreement**. Jesus said, 'If two of you…agree about anything they ask for, it will be done for them by my Father' (Matthew 18:19 NIV). When you're up against something too big to handle alone, find a prayer partner and get into agreement with them. This isn't for people who constantly live-in strife, then decide to agree because they're desperate. God honors the prayers of those who pay the price to live together in harmony (See Psalm 133:1). 6) **The prayer of thanksgiving**. When your prayers outnumber your praises, it says something about your character. Self-centered people ask, but rarely appreciate. God will not release us into the fullness of all He has planned for us until we become thankful for what we've already received. Petition avails much; praise avails much more! 'In every situation, by prayer and petition, with thanksgiving, present your requests to God' (Philippians 4:6 NIV). Powerful living comes through thanksgiving. We can literally 'pray without ceasing' (1 Thessalonians 5:17 KJV) by being thankful all day long, praising God for His favor, mercy, loving kindness, grace, longsuffering and goodness.

Day 81 – Job 4:3-4 (GNT)

Speak words that ENCOURAGE

3 You have taught many people
   and given strength to feeble hands.
4 When someone stumbled, weak and tired,
   your words encouraged him to stand.

Just an Observation

The Bible says, 'Help others with encouraging words' (Romans 14:19 MSG). When Job was in trouble, his friend Eliphaz reminded him how in the past Job's words had 'encouraged those who were about to quit'. Words can hurt or heal, bless or blister, destroy or deliver, tear down or build up. 'The tongue has the power of life and death' (Proverbs 18:21 NIV). Jon Walker writes: "You…the one with Jesus in your heart – are capable of murder. And so am I. We have the power to speak death with our words, and…the power to speak life. Perhaps you've been on the receiving end of a message meant to murder. "You're not smart enough…thin enough…fast enough…good enough…a real Christian wouldn't think such things." In a world where people are beaten up and put down, God gives you superhero power to punch through the negativity. You speak life when you say, "You matter to me. I like you just the way you are…Your life counts. You were created for a purpose. God loves you, and you're incredibly valuable to Him." You can become the voice of God's grace in the lives of others, supporting, loving, helping and encouraging them with the words that flow from your mouth.' God wants us to encourage each other, but that doesn't mean flattering or buttering people up. It means speaking words that help them to stay on their feet and keep going. What you say can give fresh hope to a friend, a relative, a neighbor, or a co-worker who's about to collapse. What a gift!

Day 82 – 2 Corinthians 12:8-10 (GNT)

Depend on God

8 Three times I prayed to the Lord about this and asked him to take it away. 9 But his answer was: "My grace is all you need, for my power is greatest when you are weak." I am most happy, then, to be proud of my weaknesses, in order to feel the protection of Christ's power over me. 10 I am content with weaknesses, insults, hardships, persecutions, and difficulties for Christ's sake. For when I am weak, then I am strong.

Just an Observation

Hindrances, hang-ups, and hurdles are God's gift to the self-sufficient. While He won't let you use your weakness as a crutch or a cop-out, He'll allow it to keep you dependent on Him. Paul wrote, 'I was given a thorn…to…keep me from becoming proud' (V. 7 NLT). Why would God keep you in touch with your limitations? To embarrass you. No, to empower you so that you can do His will. God's intention is to increase, not decrease your need for Him. Perhaps this illustration will help you. Imagine four steel rings. The first can support eighty pounds, the second sixty pounds, the third forty pounds, and the fourth twenty pounds. Linked together, what's the greatest weight the chain can support? Two hundred pounds? No, a chain is only as strong as its weakest link, so the answer is twenty pounds! And it's the same with us; we're only as strong as our weakest area. That's why we sometimes try to excuse or ignore them. But that's dangerous because relying on your own strength may win you a few victories and accolades and cause you to think you can handle everything on your own. It was because Paul was so brilliant that God permitted difficult circumstances that kept him on his knees, living in a state of forced dependence. After praying repeatedly for God to take his weakness away, Paul finally came to the place where he could say, 'I will boast all the more gladly about my weaknesses, so that Christ's power may rest on me' (v. 9 NIV). So today and every day, depend on God!

Day 83 – John 14:27 (GNT)

Peace of Mind

27 Peace is what I leave with you; it is my own peace that I give you. I do not give it as the world does. Do not be worried and upset; do not be afraid.

Just an Observation

You can control what goes on in your mind by filling it with God's Word. Not the Word you read casually, but the Word you process mentally, apply to each situation that arises, and stand on in times of crisis because you know it's your right to have the peace Jesus promised. Jesus corrected His disciples because they lost their peace of mind during a storm. He did not lose His. He was asleep in the back of the boat. So where are you today? Resting with Jesus in the back of the boat, or panicking with the others up front? Worry overwhelms you when you forget two things: (1) What the Lord has told you. Jesus said, 'Let us go over to the other side' (Mark 4:35 NIV). And once He spoke those words there wasn't a wave big enough to sink them. Anytime you're doing what God's told you to do, you may go through storms, but you won't sink. (2) Who's with you in the boat. The disciples thought they knew Jesus pretty well, but before the night was over, they were asking, 'Who is this? Even the wind and the waves obey him!' (v. 41 NIV). Has it ever occurred to you that the storm you're in right now has been permitted by God to show you that you don't have a problem He can't solve; that you're not alone, and that through this experience you'll come to know Him better? In the Amplified Bible the words of Jesus are translated like this: 'Do not let your hearts be…distressed, agitated' (John 14:1). The only power worry has over you – is the power you give it.

Day 84 – 1 Samuel 17:41-47 (GNT)
Bringing down Goliath

41 The Philistine started walking toward David, with his shield bearer walking in front of him. He kept coming closer, 42 and when he got a good look at David, he was filled with scorn for him because he was just a nice, good-looking boy. 43 He said to David, "What's that stick for? Do you think I'm a dog?" And he called down curses from his god on David. 44 "Come on," he challenged David, "and I will give your body to the birds and animals to eat."

45 David answered, "You are coming against me with sword, spear, and javelin, but I come against you in the name of the Lord Almighty, the God of the Israelite armies, which you have defied. 46 This very day the Lord will put you in my power; I will defeat you and cut off your head. And I will give the bodies of the Philistine soldiers to the birds and animals to eat. Then the whole world will know that Israel has a God, 47 and everyone here will see that the Lord does not need swords or spears to save his people. He is victorious in battle, and he will put all of you in our power."

Just an Observation

Bringing down the 'Goliath' in our life, we must stand up to them! Any problem we try to excuse or escape, we empower. After listening to Goliath's threats every day, fear gripped the hearts of God's people and they couldn't stand up to him. We must remember what God has already done for us. David recalled his victories over the lion and the bear. And we must do the same. Jeremiah said, 'This I call to mind...therefore I have hope: because of the Lord's great love we are not consumed, for his compassions never fail. They are new every morning' (Lamentations 3:21-23 NIV). The strength to deal with today's struggles comes from remembering how God helped us solve yesterday's struggles. We must cut off the giant's head. 'David...took his sword...and cut off his head...And when the Philistines saw that their champion was dead, they fled' (1 Samuel 17:51 NKJV). We need to know our enemy, study his tactics, and be willing to fight with the same level of intensity as he does. We must take what we've learned and apply it to his weak areas. And never assume he's dead when he's just dazed. If we don't cut off his head, he'll sneak up on us another day. Go for a permanent solution, not a short-term fix. Fortify yourself with prayer, renew your mind with the Word of God, and reach for the support that's available to you through your spiritual family. Above all, remember your strength doesn't lie in yourself, but in God. With God on your side, you'll win every time.

Day 85 – Job 1:8-12 (GNT)

Divine Protection

8 "Did you notice my servant Job?" the Lord asked. "There is no one on earth as faithful and good as he is. He worships me and is careful not to do anything evil."
9 Satan replied, "Would Job worship you if he got nothing out of it? 10 You have always protected him and his family and everything he owns. You bless everything he does, and you have given him enough cattle to fill the whole country. 11 But now suppose you take away everything he has—he will curse you to your face!"
12 "All right," the Lord said to Satan, "everything he has is in your power, but you must not hurt Job himself." So, Satan left.

Just an Observation

When God praised Job for his integrity, Satan replied, 'You have always put a wall of protection around him…take away everything he has, and he will surely curse you.' So, God gave Satan permission to test Job, but He placed limits on how far he could go (Job 2:6). There are times '…When the enemy comes in like a flood' (Isaiah 59:19 NKJV) … to attack your mind, your marriage, your relationship, your ministry, and anything that's born of God in your life. When that happens, Isaiah says, '…The Spirit of the Lord will lift up a standard [shield] against him' (Isaiah 59:19 NKJV). When you feel you're at breaking point and can't handle one more thing, the Holy Spirit lifts the wall of the blood of Jesus and tells Satan, 'This far and no further!' Paul says, 'We are hard pressed on every side, but not crushed; perplexed, but not in despair; persecuted, but not abandoned; struck down, but not destroyed' (2 Corinthians 4:8-9 NIV). There's a wall of protection around you. There's also a time for your deliverance. '…In the time of my favor I heard you, and in the day of salvation I helped you' (2 Corinthians 6:2 NIV). God will step in and intervene. The Psalmist said, '…When my heart is faint; Lead me to the rock that is higher than I' (Psalm 61:2 NAS). When your resources are depleted and you think you're going under for the last time, God has provided a refuge that's higher than your circumstances, a place where you're under divine protection and the enemy has no jurisdiction. All you must do is lift your eyes toward heaven.

Day 86 – Romans 10:17 (GNT)

Read God's Word - EVERYDAY

17 So then, faith comes from hearing the message, and the message comes through preaching Christ.

Just an Observation

If you are wise, when God talks, you'll listen. And He will talk to you through the Bible. The reason the Bible has outsold every other book is because it is God's Word on the issue. It takes approximately fifty-six hours to read the Bible through. If you read forty chapters a day you would complete the Bible within a month. If you read nine chapters of the New Testament each day you would complete it within thirty days. But you must read it systematically, regularly, and expectantly. When Satan attacked Him in the wilderness, Jesus quoted the Scriptures to him. That's why the Psalmist said, 'Thy word have I hid in mine heart, that I might not sin against thee' (Psalm 119:11). The book of Proverbs has thirty-one chapters. Here's an idea: since there are thirty-one days in most months, why not read a chapter in this wisdom book every day. Can you imagine what you'd learn? The Word of God will build your faith. 'Faith cometh by hearing and hearing by the word of God.' Your faith grows when you hear God speak, and it works when you do what He says. If you struggle to lead a victorious Christian life, read these words carefully: 'How can a young man cleanse his way? By taking heed according to Your word' (Psalm 119:9 NKJV). The solution for every problem is contained in Scripture. To be wise you must study it. To be strong in faith you must believe it. To be successful in life you must practice it.

Day 87 - 2 Corinthians 7:10 (MSG)

Repentance

Distress that drives us to God does that. It turns us around. It gets us back in the way of salvation. We never regret that kind of pain. But those who let distress drive them away from God are full of regrets, end up on a deathbed of regrets.

Just an Observation

The word 'repent' means to acknowledge your sin, renounce it, seek God's forgiveness, and try to live differently. It means doing an about-face turn and heading in the opposite direction. If you go twenty miles down the road in the wrong direction, it requires doing a U-turn and coming twenty miles back. At first this can seem discouraging. But it's profitable, because next time you'll think twice about where you're headed. Repentance sometimes means making restitution to others. Zacchaeus was a tax collector who got rich by overcharging people. But after he met Jesus he said, 'If I have cheated anyone, I will pay back four times as much' (Luke 19:8 GNT). God is more than willing to forgive you, but He may allow you to experience the painful consequences of your sin in order to motivate you towards obedience. 'No discipline is enjoyable while it is happening – it's painful! But afterward there will be a peaceful harvest of right living for those who are trained in this way' (Hebrews 12:11 NLT). Satan will try to tell you that you are beyond the reach of God's grace, but you're not. The Prodigal Son wasted his inheritance and ended up in a pigsty. But the day he decided to come back home, his father ran to meet him and restored him to full sonship in the family. And God will do that for you too. 'Let the wicked change their ways and banish the very thought of doing wrong. Let them turn to the Lord that he may have mercy on them. Yes, turn to our God, for he will forgive generously' (Isaiah 55:7 NLT).

Day 88 – Matthew 21:42 (NLT)

I SEE the Hand of God in it

42 Then Jesus asked them, "Didn't you ever read this in the Scriptures?

'The stone that the **builders rejected**

   has now **become the cornerstone.**

This is the Lord's doing,

   and it is wonderful to see.'

Just an Observation

Jesus said, 'The stone which the builders rejected has become the chief cornerstone. This was the Lord's doing, and it is marvelous in our eyes.' Note the word 'rejected'. The rejection of his brothers put Joseph on a path that led to the throne of Egypt and the saving of his family and his nation. How often has something happened in our life that we later realized was necessary? If we hadn't experienced this or walked through that, we wouldn't have been ready for the blessings we're enjoy now. When we begin to see the hand of God in it, we understand that what the enemy intended for our destruction, God used for our development. To be 'more than a conqueror' means we can stand up and say: 'Here's how I see it. It took everything I've been through to make me who I am and to teach me what I know. So, I choose to be better, not bitter. I trust the faithfulness of God more than ever. I've learned that if faith doesn't move the mountain, it'll give me strength to endure until tomorrow. And if it is not gone by tomorrow, I'll still believe that God is able and trust Him until He does.' Relax, rejoice; our steps are being arranged by the Lord (Psalm 37:23). He hasn't taken His eye or His hand off us, not even for a single moment. When we get through this trial, we'll realize that 'the worst thing that could have happened' was, in reality; 'the Lord's doing' and it will become 'marvelous in our eyes'.

Day 89 – Revelation 22:17(MSG)

Come and drink the Water of Life

"Come!" say the Spirit and the Bride.
Whoever hears, echo, "Come!"
Is anyone thirsty? Come!
All who will, come and drink,
Drink freely of the Water of Life!

Just an Observation

The Babylonians encircled Jerusalem and cut off its food supply. The question was, how long could they hold out? That's what the Babylonians kept wondering. But a month passed, then two, then an entire year, and still they held out. The secret of Jerusalem's survival lay in a water supply from a spring outside the city walls where Hezekiah had cut a 1,777-foot tunnel through solid rock. From there water passed under the city walls to a reservoir inside called the Pool of Siloam. Without it, God's people would have gone down in defeat. But it's not just another Bible story; there's an important lesson here for us. To live victoriously we must: know our life's true source; protect it and draw from it daily. If our security, our strength, our self-worth, or our strategy for living comes from any other source but God, the enemy can defeat us. Everything we need comes from God, so protect and nurture your relationship with Him, for it will always be the focal point of Satan's attack. A day without reading God's Word isn't merely a slip; it's a set-up for failure. Prayerlessness isn't carelessness; it's foolishness in the extreme. You might say, 'Well, I'm doing okay, and I don't pray or read the Bible very much.' Maybe you haven't reached your hour of testing yet. When that comes, without an established source to draw from you'll struggle more and succeed less. Is that how you want to live? If not, the word for you today is: 'Come and drink the Water of Life.'

Day 90 - Jeremiah 15:16 (GNT)

Promises in The Word of God

16 You spoke to me, and I listened to every word. I belong to you, Lord God Almighty, and so your words filled my heart with joy and happiness.

Just an Observation

God promises certain things to those who take time each day to get to know Him through His Word. He promises Joy. 'When your words came, I ate them; they were my joy and my heart's delight, for I bear your name, LORD God Almighty.' He promises Strength. 'Now I commit you to God and to the word of his grace, which can build you up and give you an inheritance among all those who are sanctified' (Acts 20:32 NIV). He promises Peace. 'Great peace has those who love your law, and nothing can make them stumble' (Psalm 119:165 NIV). 'If only you had paid attention to my commands, your peace would have been like a river' (Isaiah 48:18 NIV). He promises Stability. 'I have set the Lord always before me. Because he is at my right hand, I will not be shaken. Therefore, my heart is glad, and my tongue rejoices; my body also will rest secure' (Psalm 16:8-9 NIV). He promises Success. 'Do not let this Book of the Law depart from your mouth; meditate on it day and night, so that you may be careful to do everything written in it. Then you will be prosperous and successful' (Joshua 1:8 NIV). He promises Answered prayer. 'If you remain in me and my words remain in you, ask whatever you wish, and it will be done for you' (John 15:7 NIV). Joy, strength, peace, stability, success, and answered prayer – these are the things everybody wants. Don't you? Well, look no further. God has promised them to you when you spend time with Him in His Word each day.

Day 91 – John 1:22-23 (GNT)

WHO ARE YOU?

22 "Then tell us who you are," they said. "We have to take an answer back to those who sent us. What do you say about yourself?"

23 John answered by quoting the prophet Isaiah:

"I am 'the voice of someone shouting in the desert:

Make a straight path for the Lord to travel!'"

Just an Observation

"Who are you?" John 1:22 (NKJV) When asked, "Who are you?" John the Baptist replied, "The voice of one crying in the wilderness: Make straight the way of the Lord" (v. 23 NKJV). After listening to John for a while, his disciples left him to follow Christ. And that was okay with John, because he knew what he was called to do. Do you? We can only go on for so long "trying things." At some point we've got to discover what God called us to do and give ourselves fully to it. Apparently, Paul wasn't a particularly great speaker: "I came to you…timid and trembling…my message and my preaching were very plain" (1 Corinthians 2:3-4 NLT). But what Paul lacked as a speaker, he more than compensated for as a writer. He wrote the inspired word that enabled others to preach! Something so powerful was released through Paul's writings that even when they threw him in jail, he didn't ask for a lawyer or a gourmet meal because he was tired of prison food. No, he wanted paper so that he could keep writing. In fact, Paul wrote all the way to the end of his life. And because he did, lives are still being changed today. What a legacy! And all because one man discovered his calling and devoted himself to it. So, my question is: have you discovered your calling and devoted yourself to it?

Day 92 – Matthew 2:9-11 (GNT)

Do You Know Him?

9-10 And so they left, and on their way, they saw the same star they had seen in the East. When they saw it, how happy they were, what joy was theirs! It went ahead of them until it stopped over the place where the child was. 11 They went into the house, and when they saw the child with his mother Mary, they knelt down and worshiped him. They brought out their gifts of gold, frankincense, and myrrh, and presented them to him.

Just an Observation

The Wise Men couldn't have imagined humbler circumstances than those surrounding the birth of Jesus. Max Lucado paints the picture: 'The ground is hard, the hay scarce. Cobwebs cling to the ceiling…Mary looks into the eyes of her Son. Her Lord. His Majesty. At this point the human being who best understands who God is and what He's doing is a teenage girl…She remembers the angel's words, "His kingdom will never end." Majesty during the mundane. Holiness in the filth of sheep manure and sweat. Divinity entering the world on the floor of a stable. This baby had once overlooked the universe. His robes of eternity were exchanged for the rags keeping Him warm. His golden throne room abandoned in favor of a dirty sheep pen. Worshiping angels replaced with shepherds. Meanwhile the city hums; unaware that God has visited their planet. The innkeeper would never believe he'd just sent God out into the cold. And people would scoff at anyone who told them the Messiah lay in the arms of a teenager on the outskirts of their village. They were all too busy to consider the possibility. But those who missed His Majesty's arrival that night missed it not because of acts of evil or malice. No, they missed it because they weren't looking for Him!'

Day 93 – Psalm 27:14 (GNT)

Wait on the Lord

Trust in the Lord.
   Have faith, do not despair.
Trust in the Lord.

Just an Observation

The Psalmist said: 'I waited patiently for the Lord to help me, and He turned to me and heard my cry. He lifted me out of the pit of despair…He set my feet on solid ground and steadied me as I walked along. He has given me a new song to sing, a hymn of praise to our God. Many will see what he has done and be amazed' (Psalm 40:1-3 NLT.) Waiting, means trusting that God knows what He's doing; even when He doesn't give us all the details. It's in looking back that we realize; God had something better in mind for us and we weren't mature enough at that point to handle what we were asking Him for. We think we're ready, but God knows when we are. Over forty times in the Bible we're commanded to 'wait on the Lord'. Learning to wait is a test of maturity. Scott Peck writes: 'Delaying gratification is a process of scheduling the pain and pleasure of life in such a way as to enhance the pleasure by meeting and experiencing the pain first and getting it over with… It's the only decent way to live.' Waiting forces, us to accept that we're not in control. It humbles us in ways we need to be humbled. Consider the trapeze artist: for a split second, which must feel like an eternity, he or she is suspended in nothingness. They can't go back, and it's too soon to feel the grasp of the one who'll catch them. They must wait in absolute trust. You may be at that same point in your life right now. You've let go of what God called you to let go of, but you can't feel His hand catching you yet. Moses waited eighty years for a ministry that lasted forty years—two-thirds of his life was spent getting ready! Jesus spent thirty years preparing for a ministry that would last three-and-a-half years. From God's perspective, your life isn't measured by its length, but by its effectiveness and its impact for His kingdom. So, wait, and keep a good attitude while you're doing it. God won't disappoint you.

Day 94 – James 5:9 (MSG)

A Complaining Fast

Friends don't complain about each other. A far greater complaint could be lodged against you, you know. The Judge is standing just around the corner.

Just an Observation

Whatever you keep doing becomes a habit. That's why James says, '…do not complain…' Author Jon Gordon says, 'A complaining fast won't just make everyone around you happier…you'll experience more joy, peace, success and positive relationships.' So instead of complaining when things go wrong: (1) Practice gratitude. Giving thanks for three blessings every day energizes you and makes you feel happier. It's impossible to be grateful and negative at the same time. (2) Encourage others. Instead of complaining about what people do wrong, focus on what they're doing right. '…encourage…people who are afraid. Help those who are weak. Be patient with everyone' (1 Thessalonians 5:14 NCV). It's okay to criticize people's weaknesses if you balance it with three times more praise. (3) Focus on your success. Start a success journal. Every night before you go to bed, write down something great about your day. It could be an uplifting conversation…or an accomplishment you're proud of. There's truth to the old saying, 'Nothing succeeds like success.' When you focus on success you set the stage for more to follow. (4) Learn to let go. Instead of obsessing about what you can't change, focus on what you can influence. When you stop trying to control everything and place your life in God's hands, things have a way of working out. (5) Use the power of prayer. Paul says, '…pray…on all occasions with all kinds of prayers and requests…' (Ephesians 6:18 NIV). Prayer reduces stress, boosts positive energy, and promotes health. When you're under pressure, instead of complaining, plug in to God's power and recharge your batteries.

Day 95 – John 9:3(GNT)

Take it to the Lord

Jesus answered, "His blindness has nothing to do with his sins or his parents' sins. He is blind so that God's power might be seen at work in him.

Just an Observation

When Jesus encountered a blind man, His disciples immediately began to discuss the reason for the man's condition. They asked Jesus 'Was this man's blindness the result of his own sins, or the sins of his parents?' Jesus answered, '[He was born blind] so the power of God could be seen in him.' Notice four things: 1) The disciples were eager to attribute the man's problem to his sin. And Satan will try to convince you that because of your sin you're disqualified from God's grace, but you're not! God doesn't examine your past to decide your future. 2) When Jesus healed him, the neighbors were more interested in debating than celebrating and not much has changed! They started asking, "…Isn't this the man who used to sit and beg?" Some said he was…others said, "No…"' (v 8-9 NLT). 3) His healing failed the 'religiosity test' because the Pharisees said, "…This man Jesus is not from God…working on the Sabbath…"' (v 16 NLT). 4) Even the man's parents weren't free to praise God, because '…anyone saying Jesus was the Messiah would be expelled from the synagogue' (v. 22 NLT). To the neighbors he was a misfit, to church leaders he was a topic of debate, to his parents he was a social stigma, so they '…threw him out' (v 34 NIV). End of story? Thank God—No Way! 'Jesus…went and found him… [and]…said, "I came…so that those who have never seen will see…"' (vv 35, 39 TM). So instead of rehashing your problem and listening to other people's opinions, take it to the Lord in prayer. When you share it with others, the best you'll get is sympathy, but when you share it with Jesus, you'll get a solution.

Day 96 - Philippians 4:8-9 (GNT)

Are you a perfectionist?

8 In conclusion, my friends, fill your minds with those things that are good and that deserve praise: things that are true, noble, right, pure, lovely, and honorable. 9 Put into practice what you learned and received from me, both from my words and from my actions. And the God who gives us peace will be with you.

Just an Observation

Be honest, have you ever met a perfectionist who was truly happy? No, because when things must always 'be a certain way', life becomes miserable because it's constantly changing. As soon as you solve one problem, another comes along. Instead of dwelling on their blessings and being grateful, perfectionists focus on what's wrong and why they need to fix it. It may be a job they did that was less than perfect, a few pounds they need to lose, or even a disorganized wardrobe. Or it could be someone else's imperfections: the way they live their life, how they behave, or the way they look. Constantly dwelling on flaws—your own or someone else's makes it impossible to be grateful. Gratitude is at the core of happiness. Now, let's be clear; we're not talking about striving to do better. That's a good thing. We're talking about obsessing over what's wrong. There'll always be a better way to do something, but that doesn't mean you can't enjoy life the way it is right now. So, what's the cure? Catch yourself before you fall into the trap of insisting that things should be different from how they are. Stop and remind yourself that, in the absence of your judgment, everything will work out just fine. Paul says, '…in all things God works for the good of those who love him…' (Romans 8:28 NIV). Are you getting it? Gods in control AND it's okay to let go. Instead of focusing on the negative, 'think about the things that are good and worthy of praise'. When you do, you will begin to discover how wonderful life is.

Day 97 – Psalm 32:8 (GNT)

God-Ordained Vision

8 The Lord says, "I will teach you the way you should go;
  I will instruct you and advise you.

Just an Observation

Mother Teresa didn't set out searching for fame; it found her. She simply went to India, found a need no one else was meeting, heard the call of God, allowed her heart to be consumed by it, and ministered to multitudes of the world's most neglected and forgotten people in the slums of Calcutta. One of her most famous slogans was, 'A life not lived for others is not a life at all.' Let's face it; much of what we do each day doesn't seem to matter until it's evaluated as part of a larger picture. When you take the details of any given day, drop it into the cauldron of a God-ordained vision and stir it around, suddenly there's purpose, worth, adrenaline and the joy that comes from knowing you are fulfilling your destiny. It is like the difference between filling bags with dirt and building a dyke to save a town. There is nothing glamorous about filling sandbags but saving a town from the ravages of a flood is another matter entirely. Building a dyke gives meaning to the drudgery of shoveling dirt into sandbags. And it is like that with your vision. Many times, the everyday routine of life can feel like shoveling dirt. But take those same routines and view them through the lens of a God-given purpose, and suddenly everything looks quite different. Vision brings your world into focus. It brings order and purpose out of chaos. It enables you to see everything in a fresh light. And the good news is that God is the giver of visions—so ask Him for one!

Day 98 – Proverbs 3:5-8 (GNT)

Having a Vision

5 Trust in the Lord with all your heart. Never rely on what you think you know. 6 Remember the Lord in everything you do, and he will show you the right way. 7 Never let yourself think that you are wiser than you are; simply obey the Lord and refuse to do wrong. 8 If you do, it will be like good medicine, healing your wounds and easing your pains.

Just an Observation

Having a vision for your life gives you four things: (1) Passion. It makes you wake up in the morning and bound out of bed because there is something out there you love to do; something you believe in and are good at; something bigger than you; something you can hardly wait to get at. (2) Motivation. Author Richard B. Edler said: 'Safe living generally makes for regrets later. We are all given talents and dreams. Sometimes the two do not match. But often we compromise both before ever finding out. Later, we find ourselves looking back longingly to that time when we should have chased our true dreams and talents for all they are worth. Do not be pressured into thinking your dreams or talents are not prudent. They were never meant to be…They were meant to bring joy and fulfillment to your life.' (3) Direction. Vision simplifies decision-making. Anything that moves you closer to your vision gets a green light; everything else should be approached with caution. Vision brings what is important to the surface and weeds out anything that stands in your way. Without vision, good things will keep you from achieving great things. People without a clear vision are easily distracted. They've a tendency to drift aimlessly from one thing to another. They've no spiritual, relational, financial, or moral compass. Consequently, they make decisions that rob them of their dreams. (4) Purpose. Having vision is like getting a sneak preview of things to come. It says, 'If you don't show up, something important won't happen. Your life matters. Without you, what could be will not be.

Day 99 – Joel 2:28 (GNT)

The Power of Vision

28 "Afterward I will pour out my Spirit on everyone:

your sons and daughters will proclaim my message;

your old people will have dreams,

and your young people will see visions.

Just an Observation

A boy once asked Michelangelo why he was working so hard chipping away on the block of marble that would become his greatest masterpiece: David. The artist replied, 'There's an angel inside this rock and I'm setting him free.' The power of vision enables you to see a potential masterpiece in what others overlook or consider worthless. It also helps you discover things within yourself you never knew were there. It brings out the best in you. Many of the people God used in Scripture looked like losers before they looked like winners. After the disciples fished all night and caught nothing, Jesus told them, '…Do not be afraid. From now on you will catch men' (Luke 5:10 NKJV). They did, and they ended up: a) building a church that is still thriving two thousand years later; b) writing history's greatest books; c) having our sons named after them. Does that mean you can just dream a dream and God will fulfil it? No. Paul says, '…You are not your own; you were bought at a price. Therefore, honor God…' (1 Corinthians 6:19-20 NIV). At Calvary you lost the right to take your talents, opportunities and experiences and run off in any direction you please. But why would you even want to? What could possibly be more fulfilling than God's purpose for your life? And what could be more tragic than missing it? You cannot wring enough meaning out of secular accomplishments to satisfy your soul. The hole you are trying to fill has an eternal dimension only Christ can fill. That is why we must pray, 'Lord, show me Your vision for my life.'

Day 100 – Acts 17:28-29 (GNT)

Ask God

28 as someone has said,

'In him we live and move and exist.'

It is as some of your poets have said,

'We too are his children.'

29 Since we are God's children, we should not suppose that his nature is anything like an image of gold or silver or stone, shaped by human art and skill.

Just an Observation

George Washington Carver, an agricultural chemist who discovered three hundred uses for peanuts, shared these observations about God: 'As a small boy exploring the almost virgin woods of the old Carver place, I had the impression someone had just been there ahead of me. Things were so orderly, so clean, and so harmoniously beautiful. A few years later in these same woods…I was practically overwhelmed with the sense of some great presence. Not only had someone been there, but someone was also there…Years later when I read in the Scriptures, "…in Him we live, and move, and have our being," I knew what the writer meant. Never since have I been without this consciousness of the Creator speaking to me…the out-doors has been to me more and more a great cathedral in which God could be continuously spoken to and heard from…Man, who needed a purpose, a mission to keep him alive, had one. He could be…God's co-worker…My purpose alone must be God's purpose to increase the welfare and happiness of His people…Why, then, should we, who believe in Christ, be so surprised at what God can do with a willing man in a laboratory?' In 1921, Carver spoke before the United States House of Representatives. The chairman asked, 'Dr. Carver, how did you learn all these things?' He answered, 'From an old book.' The chairman asked, 'What book?' Carver replied, 'The Bible.' The chairman enquired, 'Does the Bible talk about peanuts?' Carver replied, 'No sir, but it talks about the God who made the peanut. I asked Him to show me what to do with the peanut, and He did.' Do you need a creative idea or solution today? Ask God!

My Cupcake "A Daily Tasty Treat" Devotional

"O taste and see that the LORD is good!"
Psalm 34:8

"Now that you have indulged in this devotional; you can agree the Lord is Good!"

NOTES:

My Cupcake "A Daily Tasty Treat" Devotional

My Cupcake "A Daily Tasty Treat" Devotional

My Cupcake "A Daily Tasty Treat" Devotional

My Cupcake "A Daily Tasty Treat" Devotional

Made in United States
Orlando, FL
13 September 2023